VAMPIRE WARS

THE SACRIFICE

Heather Knox

EPIC Escape

An Imprint of EPIC Press
abdopublishing.com

The Sacrifice
Vampire Wars: Book #5

abdopublishing.com

Published by EPIC Press, a division of ABDO, PO Box 398166, Minneapolis, Minnesota 55439. Copyright © 2019 by Abdo Consulting Group, Inc. International copyrights reserved in all countries. No part of this book may be reproduced in any form without written permission from the publisher. Escape™ is a trademark and logo of EPIC Press.

Printed in the United States of America, North Mankato, Minnesota.

062018
092018

Cover design by Candice Keimig
Images for cover and interior art obtained from iStockphoto.com
Edited by Jennifer Skogen

Library of Congress Cataloging-in-Publication Data

Library of Congress Control Number: 2018932899

Publisher's Cataloging in Publication Data

Names: Knox, Heather, author.
Title: The sacrifice/ by Heather Knox
Description: Minneapolis, MN : EPIC Press, 2019 | Series: Vampire wars; #5
Summary: As part of her infiltration of Project Harvest, Delilah must allow herself to become close to Victor. But the bond she's formed with him, and the truth about his work at Project Harvest, cause Delilah to question exactly why the Keepers and Praedari are at war—and to doubt the authenticity of her relationship with Zeke. Things around Project Harvest have taken a turn for the worse for the remaining captives, as an unfriendly face reappears and the Keepers' siege on the facility begins.
Identifiers: ISBN 9781680769081 (lib. bdg.) | ISBN 9781680769364 (ebook)
Subjects: LCSH: Vampires--Fiction. | War--Fiction--Fiction. | Secret operations--Fiction. | Siege warfare--Fiction | Young adult fiction.
Classification: DDC [FIC]--dc23

For Sylvia Quinn

With gratitude to
Chloe Anna for the memories,
realized & almost

1
Now

CHILLY HERE, DAMP. SMELLS OF EARTH—NOT FRESH, but acrid, like too much wet and too much time.

I hear breathing. I hear heart.

Smell of heart follows, then a grunt. The crumple of someone tossed to the ground in the probably-dark outside this coffin.

For the first time since they brought me here, I am not alone.

My reward or their punishment?

Now

WHAT THEY DON'T SEE: THE LIGHTS FLICKER SEVeral times overhead before committing to casting their fluorescent glow over the suite, illuminating the remaining captive. The sensored locks of the door click into place with finality, reinforcing the manual locks her escort had put into place upon her arrival, a precaution that until now she didn't even realize the door had. Lucky for them that they were never considered so great a threat as to need a second set of locks. Lucky for them, since this allowed them to go through with their plan after Charlie took out the back-up generator. Lucky for them—for Kiley, still here, still captive, but still unharmed. And lucky for Charlie and Logan who got away.

Unlucky, of course, for Hunter.

They see, from between two trucks in a row of vehicles at the edge of the property, the whirring-on of the power throughout the facility as windows around the perimeter light up in near simultaneity. Charlie sees the order of the current as its veins alight throughout the facility and grounds, the old silo reawakening last—senses still heightened from her time in the infirmary.

What they don't hear: footsteps retreating from the doorway of the suite they used to share, Kiley slumping to the floor, sobbing, the video monitor above her broadcasting static as an analog TV would. *Myrekrig*, as Logan would know it from his great-grandmother: Danish for "war of the ants" but he's not there. Neither of them are. They escaped.

What they hear instead: the fuzz of a radio

between stations as the truck purrs to life. Keys left in the ignition, just over half a tank of gas, headlights too dim to be legal but she clicks them off for now anyway. Charlie reaches over and turns a knob to the left, quieting but not eliminating the empty channel. She doesn't bother reversing out of the spot, instead pulling forward and through a downed part of the fence, probably what would've been her and Logan's next project out in the yard as their vampire guards looked on. She hears the click of a seatbelt, looks over to see Logan, pale and sweaty, knuckles whitening as he grips the seat.

"Are you—?" She stops when he shakes his head and rolls down his window, the old crank kind, gulping the clean air. She wants to tell him that the seatbelt will just slow them down when they're caught up to, but she doesn't.

"We—we're not going back for them, are we?" he asks after several moments pass in silence between them.

"How stupid *are* you?" Charlie snaps from the

driver's seat, surprising herself in her hostility, staring ahead at the gravel road she doesn't remember bumping down to get here.

"Charlie—" Logan starts, taken aback by her outburst, but is interrupted.

"Don't *Charlie* me. Maybe it's time Princess Kiley woke up and smelled the freakin' vampires. I grabbed you but it's not like her legs were broken. She could've run when we did but she chose not to." The words boil over as she accelerates, the truck leaving dust in their wake. A risk, kicking up so much, but intermittent glances in her rearview mirror confirm no one follows them, or no one she can *see* follows them—probably still distracted by the generator meltdown and the capture of the other two, and that Delilah woman.

"We should go back for them. Kiley first, then we can find where they took Hunter," he suggests, his tone fading to a plea when he sees the hard line of her set jaw, the tension in her hands and arms as she steers.

"Logan, Hunter is *dead*."

"You don't know that—" he starts, but his attempt at optimism is met with a glare, so he switches to a different approach. "Wherever they took him, maybe we can find him first and then go back—"

"They killed him. Don't be naive," Charlie hisses. "And I don't need a man stepping in to protect me. I don't need a knight in shining armor or whatever shielding me from the harsh reality of this. And neither does she."

Logan responds by putting his hands up in surrender but can't bite back the words that spill forth. "Kiley's right about you, thinking everything is black and white, good and evil—nothing nuanced or complicated about it. She said they *need* us."

"So say the murderous monsters of the night— and they never lie, right?" Charlie retorts, swerving to miss something dead in the gravel that they've passed before Logan even processes the existence of the shape in the moonlight, grunting something too late and unintelligible.

Despite her body language, she always comes off as ready for a fight, weight seemingly evenly distributed even as she drives. It's something Logan might not have noticed if he hadn't seen her do the dishes a million times or sort scrap out in the yard with him or stand in the doorway of the bathroom after a shower watching a newscast on the television for a few long moments trying to decide if it's genuine or fabricated and if their captors even have the capability to fabricate a news channel, and why bother?—something the four of them have debated and disagreed about at length, each landing on both sides of the argument at different times.

"If they were going to murder one of us, then what were they waiting for?" Logan challenges, unsure of his own argument even as he makes it.

"*If?!* They almost killed me! And that other girl got away, Morgan or whatever—"

"Morgeaux," Logan corrects on impulse, visibly

shrinking when her head swivels and she glares in his direction.

"*Whatever*," Charlie hisses. "Victor didn't seem too worried about sending out a search party for her. So who's to say how many of us they need alive? And anyway, wasn't it Kiley's buddy Lydia who told her they need our *blood*? I don't know about you, but I can't think of a method of blood drawing outside of a hospital that ends well for the one giving it up."

Tears glisten in Charlie's eyes but do not spill over. "Face it," she continues. "He's dead somewhere, drawn and quartered, hung like a fresh kill to bleed out. Kiley's next. And if we don't put as much distance between us and them as soon as possible, we're numbers three and—" But even as she speaks she hears a voice besides her own in the cab of the truck, muffled, broken, indistinct.

3

Now

HUNTER COMES TO SLOWLY, HIS VISION AT FIRST blurred. He brings his hand to his head where the throbbing pulses, feeling something sticky: a laceration and a hard bump protruding from his scalp, the combination leaving little room for him to imagine why he finds himself coming to in the dark. He sits up slowly, a wave of nausea rolling over him followed by that deep throbbing in his head that echoes his pulse. Deep, steadying breaths.

Underground, he knows that much: the kind of cool brought on by damp earth, the smell of a space that's never quite dried right. Petrichor, the smell of earth after it rains, may be romantic and clean, but left too long becomes a putrid combination of ammonia and rot.

Silence. Either far enough away from everything to not hear the chaos of the ranch, or far enough underground it doesn't matter. Unsure how long he was out makes it difficult to judge.

He scans the room. For the first time since being brought here, he's alone, the tension of four personalities and no walls to hide behind now leaving a sort of vacuum in his chest, an ache, a distracting rush of nothing in his ears. This, the kind of silence that makes the body cacophonous.

Slumped against a wall, head on his knees and cradled in the crooks of his elbows, Hunter sobs. It's dim, but not so dim as to really compromise his vision, some waning yellow light coming from a battery-operated Coleman lantern on a hook near the door. Though he assumes himself underground, he sees no stairs: just the windowless door sitting two or so inches off the ground, likely the result of a faulty foundation and this place settling.

The room itself is larger than the average storm cellar, maybe twelve feet by fourteen, but Hunter is certainly not ruling out that purpose for this structure. A gleaming steel pit latrine with a seat sits in one corner, a black ventilation pipe running from the base of the latrine to the wall above, going *somewhere*. Against the wall furthest from the door, and taking up most of the room, rests a plain concrete box, about seven feet long and just under three feet wide, the top fastened to the bottom by a series of heavy chains and padlocks through thick machinery eye bolts.

Mostly empty shelves line one wall, a few dusty tin cans occupying space, eight dirty jugs of distilled water line the wall underneath the shelves. On one of the shelves, a row of hotel-pristine white comforters folded with pillows on top, bedding Hunter recognizes as extras from the main house.

A bunker or a prison?

He stands and goes to the shelves. Simple metal utility shelves, rusted, held together by screws. The metal slightly sharp to the touch in places, could be used to cut into something if disassembled. Swiping a finger across the tops of a few of the cans he reads corn, beans, peas—each labeled in black marker without a date.

He leans in to the bedding and sniffs: the smell of chlorine and soft, indistinct perfume. These were probably brought down while he was unconscious, the smell of mildew not yet taken hold within the fibers.

He squats to investigate the water jugs, more there than on first glance, three rows of eight instead of just eight. He lugs one to the lantern by the door. After wiping away dirt with spit and his sleeve it appears clear in the soft light, seemingly without debris. He opens it, a seal popping. How long is distilled water good for? He sniffs and smells nothing. A tentative sip, also nothing.

A human can survive without food for up to

eight weeks as long as they have water. Each jug is a gallon, one hundred and twenty-eight ounces. Two days' worth of water per jug, forty-eight days total, though he figures maybe someone could survive on less if they had to. Shaving even two ounces a day could buy him twenty-four extra days. Just one ounce an extra twelve.

There's a way to distill urine into potable water, but he never paid that much mind, figuring if he were ever in a survival situation where he needed that knowledge he would've either already teamed up with someone as capable as himself or Googled it.

That nagging little voice inside his head admonishes him that. *Spending all that time on urban survival websites and can't do something as simple as distill urine? What good are the numbers if you can't stretch them? Does you need your mommy to come take apart a set of shelves, too? Open a can?*

He kicks the wall underneath the lantern out of frustration before noticing something strange about the door that he hadn't earlier: smooth where there should be a knob. He clicks the lantern off, stepping back to investigate the door. No light comes in along the cracks, not even along the large gap at the bottom.

He bends and puts his face to the crack where the knob should be but without backlighting cannot tell if there's a latch structure. The door is thick enough that there's a chance there is a latch and that the knob only runs through half the thickness.

He gets on his knees and lowers his chest to the ground, looking underneath the gap. He blinks several times and thinks he sees the edge of a stair. Still, no light as he looks upwards—either because it's nearly airtight or nighttime beyond.

He gets up and fumbles for the lantern turn-key, bathing the room again in warm yellow light. He once again lowers himself to the gap, this time with the lantern, looking out and upward. Unmistakable: rustic stairs of crumbling stone, cement poured in patches in quick, makeshift repair. Uneven and wet, the dark of slippery growth visible even in the pale light, these stairs weren't meant to be taken daily when they were built and haven't been repaired enough for it now. A length of wood lies along the side, probably once attached to the wall and used as a hand railing. From the gap he can't see to the top.

He stands, hanging the lantern again on its hook and returning the jug to its spot on the floor. Eyeing the blankets a moment, his attention turns to the cement—Chest? Box? Vault? He carries a pile of bedding over, setting it down on top of it.

He circles it, running his hand along the top edge. He circles it again, bent part of the way down to listen, knocking on it as he repeats his loop. It definitely opens, a lid fit onto a base, and it's definitely not meant to *be* opened. Not by him, at least, and not by anyone who would happen upon it down here. He can get his fingers underneath the lid in the narrow space but a hard tug upward confirms what he suspects: it's too heavy for him alone to budge even if the series of chains and locks has some give to it.

A primitive cooler? (But why the locks?) Food storage? (But why the locks?) Tools? (But why the locks?) A memorial vault for dead pets? (But why the locks?) Temporary interment for a baby, or children who died young, when the ground was too frozen to break with shovel? (But why the locks?)

Are the locks meant to keep someone out—or keep something in?

With that thought he takes a deep, steadying breath and bends down, placing his nose to where lid-meets-base, that narrow gap he can wedge his fingers into, and takes a deep whiff. A relieved sigh when all he smells is what he imagines concrete must smell like. A small blessing: if this held, or holds, something dead, the seal is enough to keep the smell inside.

Or it's been there long enough that decomposition is complete and the only thing that remains is bone. So, that question again: *Are the locks meant to keep someone out—or keep something in?*

No matter, for now. Maybe later he can disassemble the shelving and try to pick the locks, but for now the cement encasement will serve as his bed, keeping him up off the cold, damp ground. Sure, it's also cool and damp, but less so than the ground—and maybe whatever's inside will serve as insulation. He shudders at the thought. He lays down two comforters, each folded in half. The fold of the topmost he lines with pillows, end-to-end, a fluffy down taco filled with fluffy down pillows. The thought makes him smile.

He lays two more comforters on top of one another, then folds them likewise, making a double-layer sleeping bag of sorts. A pillow for his head. Still more bedding on the shelves so he grabs another pillow, a weird luxury all things considered. Perhaps a kindness of one of the humans on staff who knows more about his incarceration than he does. This pillow he'll hold against himself at his core, breathing into it to warm the fibers creating something of a heat pack from his own recycled breath.

He steps back, admiring his handiwork. It's probably overkill; he's not more than chilled now and that's from the damp in the air, but it's nice to feel productive. Tomorrow—today? Later he'll scrounge for anything else there might be, anything that might've rolled into a dark corner or underneath the shelves and been forgotten. And the ventilation for the latrine or the latrine itself might have useful components if he wants to risk it.

The shelves themselves will be a good resource if the screws aren't too rusted in to pry out without tools. Can opener, weapon, lockpick, sharp edge to cut fabric or carve into the cement brick walls to mark time? A way to open his veins if the quiet becomes unbearable?

His head still hurts. He removes the lantern from the hook where it hangs, carrying it with him to his new bed. Click. He climbs into the makeshift sleeping bag, unsure how long he was unconscious and without a way right now to see whether it's night or day. He closes his eyes. *Are the locks meant to keep someone out—or keep something in?* He takes a deep breath, holds it, and listens. *Maybe they have a pet. Maybe it's something even* they're *afraid of.* He exhales, laughing to himself in the darkness.

But he can't stop the question from following him into his slumber.

Are they trying to keep someone out—or keep something in?

4

Now, and Then

A SOFT KNOCK AT MY DOOR NOT LONG AFTER THE lights flicker on. I know who stands on the other side but I do not call to him. Another knock, then:

"Delilah, I'm coming in," and the whoosh of the doors opening.

I stand from my bed to greet him, unsure of what this greeting should even look like. My eyes fall to what he holds: my bag, taken by Liam and Mina when they captured me.

"I wanted to bring you this," Victor explains, taking a few steps farther inside and offering the bag out to me. "I can't promise that anything of value is still in there, but your personal effects were likely left alone. If you had cash you probably don't anymore."

"Thanks," I say with a small smile, taking my bag and setting it on my bed to go through later.

"They're all provided for here, at the ranch, in exchange for their help—but old habits die hard. Not that every Praedari is a hardened street thug, either, but . . . well, a lot of them have had rather 'eat or be eaten' lives until now. But I suppose you already know that . . . " he pauses, cocking his head slightly as if studying my reaction.

Phantom breath catches in my throat. Does Victor mean my time undercover with Zeke, infiltrating the Praedari? We took measures to clean up after the raid, with the help of the Council, but I've always wondered whether that was enough.

He continues: "I mean, being raised a Keeper, that's your view on the Praedari, right?"

I shrug, taking a seat on the edge of my bed.

"Some. Most that I've come across. Lydia certainly seems to fit that stereotype. Liam and Mina seemed . . . different, though."

I pick up my purse and quickly inventory the contents by touch. My wallet, probably emptied. Lipstick, mirrored compact, a pen, some crumpled up receipts, a set of keys. The hole in the corner of the lining that started out as a tear and grew to a size that could swallow most anything. Through the lining I feel something like a small box. I frown.

"What is it?" Victor asks, taking a seat on the bed next to me.

"My phone is gone."

"Yeah, someone'll probably sell that. Sorry. We keep cellular signals jammed here anyway for security reasons, so it wouldn't have done you much good except as an alarm clock."

"And I'm missing a book."

"Sentimental value?" he asks, concerned.

"No," I shake my head. "Just a copy of *We Have*

Always Lived in the Castle. I was getting towards the end."

He laughs. "You always did have a book in hand. That'll probably turn up. I can order you another if you like? Amazon—it'll be here in like two days."

I shake my head again, my fingers tripping on something that doesn't belong. Metal.

"What is it?" Victor frowns. "Is something else missing?"

"No, actually . . . " I withdraw my hand from my purse, holding up two rugged metal hoops, silver in color and thicker than what I'd wear as a bracelet, with a wider diameter and a gap in the hoop itself. Each inscribed with runes and simple symbols inside and out, similar but not identical. "These aren't mine."

"I put those in there. They belonged to—"

"—Liam and Mina. I remember them. They wore them up here, on their bicep," I say, demonstrating with my hand around my arm.

"Viking arm bands," Victor explains. "Mina

explained it to me once as a tradition in their family, pledging their loyalty to their lineage above all else. It would actually be seen as somewhat heretical by the sect but their family predates the divide and has never given the Praedari reason to question which side they serve."

"Why are you giving them to me?"

"They broke rank by dragging you into that rite. Delilah, you *know* me. Do you honestly think I care that much about some forced sense of hierarchy? I'm the alpha of this place to maintain appearances and to give the others something they're familiar with—and to protect what I'm building here."

Know, knew. Does it matter if I've forgotten? But I do not say this. Instead I fidget with one of the rings, turning it through my fingers. All that's left of two lives, their ashes now scattered by wind or left to wash into the soil with the next rainfall. I guess this happens with mortals, too, flesh and muscle and bone in a silk-lined casket buried in the earth. There's something comforting about that containment, something permanent about the structure containing them.

"Delilah?"

"Hmm?" I startle, jarred from my thoughts.

"It's a token of good faith. Like this," he says, producing a key card from his breast pocket. "Here."

"What's this?"

"It'll give you access to some of the facility—anything that doesn't require a higher security clearance, of course. With this you can walk out that front door. All of our vehicles have keys in the ignition—we're not worried about theft this far out. You can go and never look back, if that is your wish. I'll see you to safety myself, if that is your wish. Delilah, I know you didn't believe me before, but you're not a prisoner here. No one is—not you, not the kids, not our donors."

Donors? But I do not ask. Instead, my guilt gets the better of me: "What about the tall kid you had taken away?"

Victor only smiles. "I think you'd like it here once you settle in. Just give me a chance to convince you? Maybe—" he reaches out and tucks a lock of hair behind my ear and I notice for the first time that the predator within me still sleeps. "Maybe for old times' sake?"

"I could go and never look back?" I ask softly, my eyes locking with his.

"Yes, but first . . . "

♧

When his lips meet mine the earth underneath me gives way for just a moment and I'm tumbling, the smell of mountain air: pine and the sweet of wildflowers. A window yawns open. A bee buzzes outside. We're laughing. I catch my reflection in a mirror above the dresser, my dark curls wild. I smooth them with one hand.

"Stop. You're beautiful." Victor places two

fingers under my chin and tilts my head up. "Always," his lips whisper against mine.

"You're so full of it," I tease, my lips still brushing his.

He laughs, then pulls me in for a kiss, half-propping up and fumbling behind me for something underneath the pile of open notebooks, highlighters, a calculator, an open math textbook that's dingy on the edges, seen better days.

"What's that?" I ask, trying to see what he's grabbed when the kiss ends, but he's fast and hiding it behind his back.

"I don't love you because you're beautiful, you know."

"Well, that's a heck of a thing to tell a girl!"

"No," he laughs. "I mean, yes, you're beautiful—but you're so much more than that. You're smart—you've read like every book they say you should read before you die."

"You're not faring any better here—" He puts his finger to my lips to shush me, smiling.

"You stand up for yourself. Remember when that jerk from English class junior year—"

"Tyler Kingston."

"—remember when he pretended to fall against you, shoving you into the bookcase at the back of the room? And when he did he grabbed your hair? You grabbed him by the arm and what was it you said? 'If I catch you bothering anyone else—'"

"'—I'm tearing this off and feeding it to you,'" we say in unison with a laugh.

"You stand up for others, too. I wouldn't say you're *wildly* popular—"

"I'm flattered."

"Let me finish! You're *definitely* not popular—"

"Laying that charm on thick . . ." I tease.

"But you're *you*. And people notice that. They find themselves drawn to you, whether they're afraid of you or in love with you."

I scoff. "Yes, I'm beating droves of potential suitors off with a stick."

"Maybe not *romantically* in love with you,"

32

he clarifies, "but you have something that makes people want you, or want to be you. You're passionate. You're confident. You're not afraid of anything, but you have this depth, this softness there that if someone earns it, you let them in. You don't do anything halfway, and I don't want to, either. Delilah . . . "

"Delilah? Are you okay?"

His fingers brush my cheek, his gray eyes full of concern. As I come to, I find that I'm whispering and looking around. I'm lying down but there's no smell of pine or sweet of wildflower, instead sterile like a hospital or car dealership showroom, bleach and leather. I'm in his arms in this bed I could bounce a quarter off of, with its hotel-crisp sheets and white everything, not white like literally the color, but the feeling. I wince at the bright of the fluorescent lights overhead.

"Hey, I'm sorry." He shakes his head, sitting up. "I shouldn't have—I should've asked first. It's been so long, I shouldn't have assumed . . . "

"No! No, it's not—the kiss was fine, good. I liked it. I mean—it was welcome." I reassure him, sitting up and putting my hand on his shoulder, realizing just how crazy I probably seem—fully lucid one moment and wide-eyed and muttering the next.

"Yeah?"

I nod. "I just—"

"Went somewhere else a moment?"

I nod again, furrowing my brow in concentration. "Yeah, something like that."

"I find myself doing that now that you're here. Feelings rush back, ones that I had to repress when I died because . . . because it wouldn't be fair to you if I came back after my Becoming."

"I thought you were dead," I accuse. A tear rolls down my cheek and I'm quick to wipe it away—but not quick enough.

"I was scared," he admits. "I'm sorry. I shouldn't have taken that choice from you."

"You were going to propose."

"I'm sorry?"

"You were going to propose but we were interrupted. There was a bee buzzing outside an open window. We were doing homework—"

"Going to propose?" He takes my hand in his, concern again clouding his eyes. He speaks softly, as if the truth might break me. "Delilah, you said yes. We were engaged."

5

Before

"WILL ANYONE COME LOOKING FOR YOU?"
Zeke asks again, as he has nearly every
night since my Becoming, or so it seems.

"Worried you'll have competition?" I joke.

He frowns. "It's hard to die without a grave."

"History would beg to differ."

"I mean it's hard to stay missing if someone
wants you found. I'm serious, Delilah. You're young
enough that you can pass as still alive—if you get
pulled over for speeding a cop isn't going to question your driver's license—but that means you're

also young enough that you might find yourself recognized when you'd rather not be remembered."

"I've told you—" I sigh, but am interrupted.

"I know," he starts, taking my hands in his. "And I'm going to keep asking, every night if I have to, because maybe you'll remember something. And I know you *want* to remember. Besides," he reaches up with one hand to twirl one of my dark curls in his fingers. "I have a hard time believing you're not leaving anyone special behind."

Now

"**I** SAID, WHERE ARE THE OTHER TWO? CHARLIE? Logan? Did you leave them behind?" A woman's voice crackles over the radio.

"They found us!" Charlie shrieks, clicking the radio off as if it might somehow act as a spyglass for their captors. "That's gotta be Delilah!"

"What the—?" Logan stares at the radio, brushing her hand aside to turn the radio back on.

"Stop! They'll track us!" But unless they went to great lengths to hide GPS in the primitive radio of the truck, she knows it's unlikely.

"I don't think it's them, they wouldn't ask us that. Would they?"

"I'm not *them*," says the mysterious voice. "Don't turn me off."

"Is—is the truck talking? Like in that old show *Knight Rider?*" Logan guesses. Charlie flashes him a look and sighs deeply, focusing again on the uneven road, not even sure what direction she heads in but they've found pavement, at least. She rubs her temple.

Then the woman speaks again. "I'm not the truck. It's a long story, but I'm an ally. You need to trust me."

A pause as Logan and Charlie exchange looks, then another voice: "Me too! I'm a friend, too. My name's Morgeaux. They tried to bring me to— wherever you just got away from. The other voice is Quinn, she helped me."

"Morgeaux?!" Logan and Charlie ask in unison.

"The one that got away!" Logan elaborates.

"Yes. But only because Quinn and that other lady rescued me. Quinn's a vampire but—"

Charlie narrows her eyes. "But she's the good kind!" she mocks.

"Well, no. She's—she's not like the ones out there, the ones bombing and killing and—"

Charlie cuts her off. "I'm not trusting another vampire. That Keeper is why Hunter's being punished."

"Delilah?" The first woman, Quinn, asks over the radio. "I would've checked in on her but it was too risky. She has her part to play in all this."

"She's the other woman that saved me!" Morgeaux adds. "Look, don't trust Quinn, fine. But meet with me. Please. I need to see who you are."

"No way," Charlie shakes her head as though they can see. "You could be another one of them for all we know."

"Charlie . . . " Logan pleads, placing his hand on her forearm which still grips the wheel.

"No!" she snaps. "No way. How are they even *on* this radio if they're not tapping in from the ranch?"

"We're in the shadow-space between worlds," the woman called Quinn explains, uninvited. "Morgeaux is only here because she requested I bring her to come find you as soon as I saw you'd escaped, but I am no stranger to this in-between." She sighs when she's met with silence. "A few minutes ago you swerved to avoid what you thought was roadkill. It wasn't. It was a raven—much like the one you'll see in your rearview mirror if you look now."

Charlie's eyes dart to the mirror and she gasps, the minor distraction allowing the vehicle to dip momentarily beyond the white line to the shoulder. Logan cranes his neck in his seat. Sure enough, there in the bed of the truck a big black bird pecks at some stray straw.

"You're . . . the raven?"

"Not this time, no. The raven is a messenger,

though sometimes I ride them myself—and rarely become one."

"If you were there to see us escape, why not *help* us escape?" Logan asks, staring at the raven through the back window. "With help, Kiley and Hunter could have—" but he can't finish the thought, only shaking his head.

"Too many of them, an infestation. We must restore the balance, but we must not meddle."

"Drop me off." Morgeaux's request crackles over the radio, startling Charlie who'd nearly forgotten she was there. "Drop me off in the real world somewhere and leave me to meet them."

"Morgeaux, that's not safe. Not with everything going on out there—"

"I need to meet them. We're related. Kind of. At least in this we are. And they don't know what they're stepping in, what's gone down since they left. You can't meddle but I sure can."

7

Now

"**Y**OU HONESTLY DON'T REMEMBER?" VICTOR'S tone walks that fine line between curious and accusatory.

I shake my head. "None of it." I want to ask if this is just how it is for some Praedari, since I was made *like* a Praedari, but I don't want to raise a red flag. Instead I say, "Maybe that's just how it is for some Everlasting." I leave the wording of it as open-ended as I'm able. "Maybe some of us don't remember what came before our Becoming."

It's his turn to shake his head. "I've never heard of the Becoming bringing about amnesia.

43

Temporarily, sure, like a symptom of shock or PTSD—but not long-term, and certainly not your entire life, who you *are*, disappearing from memory. What you're talking about . . . " his words trail.

"What?"

"The Keepers having Binding Ritae." He preempts my attempt at double talk with a wave of his hand. "It's not a secret. It's not a well-kept secret, at least. Some Praedari come to the sect after being Ushered by a Keeper and finding that it's not a good fit—we accept them with open arms, partially because they bring with them knowledge about Keeper culture."

"That's awful trusting," I quip.

"Oh, we have our own version of the Binding Ritae and transfers from your sect aren't exempt from them."

Of course, I know this, and the Keepers do, too. That's why the Council demands Ushers keep their Children in their tutelage before granting them Autonomy, and doing so is a formal process, documented and sanctioned by the Council itself. If a newly made Everlasting leaves the safety of their Usher's nest before their time, you can bet they'll be hunted down, along with their Usher. The Keepers make quick work of deserters.

"What I'm saying," he continues, "is that it sounds a bit like tampering to me. Like someone didn't want you to remember. Maybe someone who did your Binding Ritae?"

"You mean my Usher. Zeke. You think Zeke tampered with my memory? On purpose?"

Victor puts his hands up, as if to deflect the questions. "I'm saying 'what if?' And if we're asking 'what if?' maybe we should also be asking 'why?'"

"Well, I'm not."

"Not what?"

"Asking! It's crazy. There's no way—besides, I've remembered enough of my Becoming to know that when I—" When I climbed from the dirt like the other Praedari I was buried with, I want to say, but can't. "When I *came to* I didn't remember who I was or how I got there."

"Sure, but that's the kind of stuff that comes back after the initial shock of it wears off." He furrows his brow, studying me. "Your experience sounds an awful lot like some of the Praedari here."

A familiar clenching in my throat joins the heaviness in my gut, like a boulder weighing down rational thought. Action and reaction claw their way from the pit of my gut, scrambling over the boulder in a desperate effort to spill out of this body first.

"Talking to some of them might help," Victor continues, and I'm almost certain the relief I'm overcome with is palpable. "Not now, of course, but if you decide to stay a while, which I hope you will. Give me a chance to show you what I've been working on. And then, when your presence isn't so new to them, they might open up." Then, as though sensing my discomfort, he says, "But look, I didn't ask you here to dredge all of that up. I thought you might like some proof of what we talked about."

He hands me a large, tattered shoebox that, according to the half-torn label now faded, once held a pair of winter boots. I move my hand to flip open the top but his hand covers mine. "Bring it with you. Look through it when you're alone." He looks into my eyes. "You have a right to everything in there."

Now

"I've stalled as long as I can, Caius. My hands are tied," Temperance explains in a frantic whisper.

"Why are they pushing this? Ezekiel is already dead. Delilah is on some wild goose chase for closure and I have a hard time believing the Council merely wishes for her to find that."

Still, Caius has to admit, even just to himself and even just in this moment, that he delights in seeing the Siren squirm. In all the time he's known her, Temperance has never so much as raised her voice, has never come across as anything other than in control of herself and everyone around her—save for this situation with Delilah. That girl knows how to get under everyone's skin without even trying, he muses; probably why Ezekiel fell for her in the first place.

"I can't tell you their intent with the girl, only that I wish her safe return just as much as you do," Temperance tries to reassure.

"You *can't* tell me their intent, or you won't?" But his question is met with silence. "Forgive me if I find that hard to believe, Siren."

"Look, I have to get inside before the others question why I'm late. Just please trust that I've taken precautions to make sure we can find her location."

"You're tracking the girl?" he barks, his tone more hostile than he intends.

"Well," Temperance sighs. "Not right at this precise moment, no."

"Meaning?"

"Meaning that if Delilah would open the gift I

sent with her, we would be able to find her location *and* determine if she needs our assistance."

"So the Council's intent is to use her as a spy against the Praedari without her consent or knowledge?" Caius demands, his voice rising as his inner predator growls awake.

"Caius, please, let's not be overdramatic." Temperance reaches to put her hand on his chest but he snatches her wrist. If she is surprised, she does not show it, not so much as a gasp crossing the threshold of her lips as her features harden and her eyes narrow to glare at him.

"Don't," he growls. "You intentionally placed that girl in harm's way—"

"Please," she scoffs. "That girl only knows how to *be* in harm's way. Just like her Usher, she was born into the fray. She's the eye of the storm, Caius."

His grip on her wrist tightens. "If anything happens to her I'm coming for you first."

Her inner beast rises to meet his with a snarl,

her fangs extending. She tries to wrench free her wrist but is no match for his strength. She thrusts her head forward, hoping to smash her skull into his nose but in one deft move he catches her by her throat, holding her up on the tips of her toes by both her throat and wrist.

With another louder growl he shoves her backwards, her head meeting something cool and hard with a sickening thud and the *tink*-crackle of glass. She stares after him as he storms up the stairs leading down to the Council chambers where they're expecting her. Drawing herself again to her full height, she turns to survey the damage the Conqueror left in his wake.

The glass protecting one of the paintings curated by Aleister now cracked: a spiderweb of crackle now obscuring the woman who stands over the recently dead on a nighttime battlefield, no light save for a faintly glowing aura and eyes aglow that seem to follow Temperance's gaze. The woman bloodied and wearing bloodied tatters, the grass and dirt soaked in the crimson dew of the slain, even the woman's headdress of raven skulls and feathers boasts droplets so crisp Temperance can nearly smell the nectar, her fangs extending again, this time in hunger. How long since she's hunted?

She's stopped to gaze upon this painting more times in the last few decades than she could count but still she can't seem to recall whether there used to be a wisp of light trailing from one of the corpses to the blade of the woman's sword, or whether those were always the tattoos marking the woman's pale skin. Did a full moon cast its glow over the slain, illuminating the eternal *oh*'s of their mouths, their sunken eyes, the waxen blue-gray of dead flesh?

"Temperance? Do you care to join us?" Leland smiles, though his tone undermines the expression, cutting through her reverie and startling her. She retracts her fangs on instinct.

"Oh! Of course. My apologies—" she brushes

past him and into the Council chambers, smiling at those already gathered. "I caught myself again admiring your painting of the Valkyrie, Aleister. Exquisite." She lets him take up her hand and kiss it, a sign of appreciation of her compliment. Taking her seat, Temperance continues: "It seems that brute, Caius, lost his temper and cracked the glass." She allows herself a sigh punctuated by a brief pout.

Leland clears his throat, visibly annoyed that she has charmed the group. They should have been annoyed by her tardiness, but he is the only one who is upset. Him and maybe Enoch, whose face remains expressionless.

"I believe it was Evelyn who called this emergency meeting of the Council of Keepers?" Leland announces in his formal way. "So I shall hand the floor over to her," he explains with a nod in her direction as he takes his seat.

Evelyn stands to address the rest of the Council. Wrinkles mar her usually crisp-pressed button-down, now coming half-untucked, an extra button undone at her clavicle revealing perhaps more skin than anyone on the Council has ever seen Evelyn reveal. Her skirt bears similar wrinkles, as though slept in, and wisps of hair frame her face. The crest pin on her lapel rests sideways. Temperance doubts she's slept much in days, if at all—especially taxing on one of the Everlasting, and impossible for most.

"We've unearthed the ritual for awakening a Slumbering Elder against their will—" she barely starts before she's interrupted.

"Were you leading the excavation team?" Brantley quips with a smirk from his place beside her. He takes his feet off the table and leans forward, putting his hand up as though his speaking to her would be a private aside but it's audible to all. "Perhaps you could've cleaned yourself up before addressing this Council—"

More than one audible gasp as the back of Evelyn's hand connects with Brantley's cheek, the slap of flesh-on-flesh thick in the air between them as his head snaps momentarily to the side with the force. Temperance smiles approvingly. Leland stifles a laugh with his hand, pretending it was a cough. Aleister claps slowly, nodding. Enoch, of course, still as stone. A shocked Brantley rubs his cheek, glaring at Evelyn, muttering under his breath no doubt a colorful array of insults that she ignores.

"Would you dare address me that way were I a man?" she demands. Then Evelyn turns her attention again to the Council. "As I was saying," she continues, pushing her shirt sleeves up off her wrists and onto her forearms. "'Against their will' may not be entirely accurate. 'Without their intending to wake' or 'before their time' may be more precise, but I suppose that's just semantics. The outcome is the same: an Elder wakes up without necessarily consenting, which is obviously dangerous for a host of reasons. This is the ritual our informants believe the Praedari to have acquired about the time they began hunting for the body of Ismae the Bloody."

"If they've had it that long why are we only now acquiring it ourselves?" Aleister inquires, carefully, Temperance notices, to keep the judgment expressed by his words out of his tone, at the very least, for fear of Evelyn's rebuke.

"I didn't say *we* had just acquired it, I said we *unearthed* it. 'To discover something hidden, lost, or kept secret by investigation or searching.' We've had the ritual in our vaults for quite some time, since well before Ezekiel's death and, therefore, well before the Praedari acquired it, but were unable to understand it until the translation was complete—which is to say that the secrets hidden behind the original text were not *discovered* until quite recently."

"I see," he says, again weighing his words against the unpredictability of Evelyn's likely-exhausted state. "But doesn't that mean that they've been sitting on a translated text longer than we have?"

"Not likely," Evelyn starts. "Long ago, ritualists among the Everlasting were hesitant to commit their spells and rituals to paper, for fear their magic could be stolen from them. To an extent they were correct: any one of you could break into my personal library and *try* to work a ritual from one of my texts. But what they didn't understand—and maybe what we still don't—is how our own will shapes the magic we work. Any who've Ushered have worked magic: we exist by a magical transfusion of blood. The Binding Rite, no matter what form it manifests in your tradition, is magic. Our *blood* is magic given physical form."

Temperance can feel the eye rolls and groans from her fellow Council members, though no one dare roll their eyes or groan out loud. The Keepers honor the Ritae, but as a matter of tradition rather than faith. Very few consider them to be literal magical rituals with a mystical element. Still, she finds it difficult to entirely discount the possibility, having Ushered as many as she has, having enjoyed the feeling of another's fangs in her flesh as often as she has. No matter how much it all sounds like nonsensical new-age hooey when put into words, there's no denying that something about their blood *is* powerful. They've been blessed with the gift to grant life beyond life, who is she to deny what elevates them above the mortal masses?

Seemingly unaware of her peers' skepticism, or so used to it by now that she hardly notices, Evelyn continues. "Now, the difficulty of translating a long-dead, primarily oral language tradition aside, the original ritual is filled with outdated parlance and nuanced figurative speech—some metaphor, idiomatic expressions, even some references to ancient literary works—that had stumped our own scholars for centuries. Even now we can't be entirely sure that our translation is faithful to the original, nor can we be sure that the original included all of the necessary information for the working of the ritual."

"So how are we any better off after your

apparent binge of all-dayers?" Brantley asks. Temperance swears she sees his eye twitch in anticipation of being backhanded again, but Evelyn takes a few seconds to honestly consider the question.

"We can be reasonably sure that our translation is more accurate than theirs," she answers, honest but noncommittal.

"Why?"

"Because I worked on it myself." She shrugs.

"Couldn't we just try it out on one of us? We're all Elders here," Leland suggests.

Evelyn gives him a look usually reserved for kindergarteners whose works of art their parents can't decipher so instead of any specific praise they receive a canned 'It's lovely, honey' and a pitying sort of glance as their parents hang it on the fridge next to a dozen others. Then she answers. "We all want it to work so if it does, we can't be sure it wasn't the will of the one Slumbering that made them awaken."

"Well you know *I* don't want you to be right,"

Brantley offers with a shrug and a sly smile. Temperance has to give him credit: he's not wrong.

"And as much as I would love to tear out your heart and put you down like the sneering mutt you are, it's not practical," she snaps at Brantley before she turns her attention to the Eldest among them seated at the head of the table. "I am hoping that you might take a look at it, Enoch, and let me know if there's anything you would change. Some of the more ancient phrases have rather nuanced meaning depending which century the amanuensis . . . " She pauses, looking to Brantley and speaking slowly, her mouth moving to over-form each word. "That means *scribe*, the one who took down the dictation. The one who wrote the words down." Then she turns her attention again to Enoch. "We can't do much better than guess at the meaning based on linguistic context. And even that's assuming they didn't go out of their way to obscure as they wrote it out."

Enoch merely offers a tip of his head as answer.

Evelyn pulls a manila folder out of her briefcase and sets it down on the mahogany table in front of Enoch. Glancing around the table at the others, Temperance notices the rather glassy-eyed stares of her peers on the Council. Her own expression might match theirs if she didn't find their subtle, likely subconscious mannerisms so fascinating. Like how Brantley hasn't relaxed since being slapped by Evelyn, though the red on his cheek faded within a minute. Or how Leland shifts his weight in his seat every few minutes, waiting for a pause in the proceedings that he may organically take back the spotlight as host. Or how Aleister purses his lips in disappointment every time Evelyn expresses a quantity of knowledge that's less than certainty. Or how Evelyn herself relishes this time in the spotlight as their resident expert even though in regular Council proceedings she only speaks up the exact amount that etiquette dictates she should. Likewise, Temperance notices the satisfaction

Evelyn takes in publicly admonishing Brantley without consequence.

But Enoch, stoic Enoch, Enoch with his silence and his leviathan presence—she cannot read, nor does she expend a great deal of effort trying, afraid what reaction she might evoke if she was caught.

"What can we do in the meantime?" Leland asks.

"We know they have some version of this ritual, and that it might work, and that they have the body of Ismae the Bloody," Brantley chimes in. "It seems to me that we should preempt their attack."

"Attack?"

"You think she's gonna wake up and throw us a party?"

"The kid has a point," Aleister agrees. "But how can we organize a strike if we're not sure where we're striking?"

"I gave the girl the trinket," Temperance says in Evelyn's direction. Evelyn nods.

"Do you care to fill the rest of us in, Siren?"

Aleister asks with a chuckle, her nickname rolling off his tongue affectionately rather than with the venom of the Conqueror. They've long been allies, even friends at times.

"Evelyn created something of a magical tracking device that, once activated, will give us her location and some insight into her surroundings and state of mind."

"Is that a pretty way of saying you are using her for surveillance without her knowledge?" Brantley asks. "But why? She spent so much time infiltrating the Praedari with Zeke that she'd probably jump at the chance to do it again, especially if she knew we were considering her for his *vacated* position on the Council."

"I—we—are interested in the *reality* of what's happening with the Praedari where ever she is, not her *perception* of what's happening with the Praedari wherever she is. She knows she's acting as an agent of this Council, but if she knew she had active surveillance it might influence her behavior."

"You mean you don't trust her," Brantley says, leaning back in his chair and crossing his arms. "Which is probably the first thing we've agreed upon in a decade." He puts his feet up on the table, crossing his legs at the ankle.

"Temperance, with your insight into matters of the heart—do you know something you're not telling us?"

"Isn't that our way, Aleister dear?" she purrs. "The problem is she hasn't activated the device," she explains with a sigh. "All she needed to do was touch it. I mean, who receives a gift and doesn't so much as open it?" Temperance pouts.

"Well, we can't just sit here and hope her curiosity gets the best of her," Brantley admonishes.

"She's her Usher's Childe. It will," Evelyn interjects with surprising calm.

"We don't even know if she has it with her, do we?" Aleister challenges.

"This is what happens when you trust the witch . . . " Brantley mutters. "What's our backup plan? Wait another century? Wait until Ismae the Bloody comes banging on our front door?"

"Give the girl time," Temperance suggests. "You don't know what she's up against there."

"Or where *there* is. Or if she's even alive." This time Brantley's commentary is met with nodding from Leland and Aleister.

Temperance, feeling a win slipping away from her, decides to reveal her hand. "Delilah is not the only agent I have in place at their facility."

Her hand, or a lie. She'll never have to tell: if it's a lie and she's wrong, Ismae the Bloody will awaken and destroy them all before the Council has time to hand down a punishment. If it's her hand and she truly does have another agent at the facility, then what harm revealing it now, behind the closed doors of the Council chambers?

Enoch studies her, unblinking. *Clever girl.* She straightens in her seat at his voice in her head, a movement the others will no doubt interpret as confidence, as her having this ace up her sleeve that no one could've guessed at—if they notice her at all as they buzz amongst themselves like bees in a hive, going in circles.

The truth is he doesn't care. It matters little to him, one way or the other.

It will all unfold as it must.

*[Evelyn's notes for Unnumbered Ritual, as transcribed
on this day by Nikolai Lockheart.]*

HEY, KEEP THE DATE OUT OF THE TRANSCRIPTION,
but it's in my handwritten notes. I'll explain
why in person.

So Nikolai, the first thing I need to explain as
you're transcribing this for me is that this ritual is to
remain unnumbered because it's actually numbered
Before the One, but there's no Roman numeral for
that number and I've thought about calling it Ritual
Negative One, but that sounds so pretentious and

anyway, it's inaccurate because negative one doesn't really come before one, I mean it does but [incoherent]. Zero might work, but again, it's not accurate. Zero is nothing, less than something, and before the one isn't nothing, it's just . . . it just *predates* the one.

We're translating this ritual that's meant to awaken an Elder against their will—which isn't really accurate, it's more like "waking them before they thought they wanted to be woken up when they originally went to sleep" or, like, "waking them without their assistance" which goes back to the idea that Elders, while Slumbering, maintain awareness of their surroundings in a sort of trance-like state. It's more like [incoherent]. Honestly, no matter how I word this it doesn't sound right except by using the direct translation: Rebirthing the Elder.

I've been awake for a week. Wait, is that possible? Do you know what it feels like to be writing this while the sun burns away in the sky and the mortals all zip to work in their carpool lanes and drop their children off at daycare, I mean of course some mortals work during the night—graveyard shift and all that—but most don't, right?

These notes aren't going to make any sense later, sorry, Nikolai. I'd say you'll understand someday, but let's hope you don't hahahaha hahahahaha. I really want to open the shades and *see* the sun, it's been so long, but I guess that's a danger of [incoherent], of going mad. Am I going mad?

I guess that's not really the question. The question is: can I *come back* from going mad? Maybe that's the intent of this ritual, the intent of the amanuensis for his master, to convolute it just enough as he copied it down that anyone trying to work it in the future would lose something of themselves, at the very least, and quite possibly all of themselves. Or at least all credibility. I'll have to pull myself together long enough to present to the rest of the Council—who, let's face it, couldn't understand magic if [incoherent].

But they'll be polite, stare politely as everything

I say goes over their simple little heads. Simple-minded fools, and still they won't want to upset the ritualist because for all they know I might come back here and burn it all to the ground or step out into tomorrow's sunrise. Ash, ash, ash . . .

Rebirthing the Elder! I forgot where we were. Okay. So this is the second ritual, the first ritual allows the Elder to enter the Slumber. We have a version of this in our vault, translated, and it's been used with great efficacy for centuries—but this one is different, married to Rebirthing the Elder, part of a set. My theory is that by using this version— the one I'm going to detail in a moment—to enter the Slumber one must use Rebirthing the Elder to awaken. Likewise, if one uses the ever-changing, ever-evolving (dare I say, *free for all*), *vulgar* contemporary version, Rebirthing the Elder would not awaken them . . . for fairly obvious reasons once I lay out the basics. Hahaha haha I say *vulgar* but the contemporary version is the one *I* would use, again for reasons that'll be obvious in a moment.

The companion ritual to Rebirthing the Elder, the one that allows them to enter the Slumber, requires removing one's heart and lung. The Elder, of course, will live as long as their heart is not pierced with wood or placed in sunlight—you know, The Big Two. I said *of course* and it makes sense biologically—the heart and lung, and all once-viable organs of the Everlasting, are dead. We are dead. We have no heartbeat and we need not breathe. And yet, the idea of removing these . . . think about it, Nikolai. If I told you I was going to remove my heart and lung, you would think me mad. But . . . here it is, in writing. (Where I'm looking, not what you're transcribing which could be utter rubbish and you'd have no idea haha hahaha hahahaha.)

According to the supplementary research conducted in tandem with this pair of rituals, Everlasting used to Usher and keep their Children as thralls so . . . wait, I'm ahead of myself.

Rebirthing the Elder, then, requires that the

Elder—who has removed their heart and lung—to be awoken needs a heart and a lung. Simple! Ha hahahaha hahahahahaha. Their own or that of another. That's where the thralls come in: Everlasting used to Usher Children to keep as thralls should they decide to undertake this ritual. These thralls would then retrieve the Elder's heart and lung, which obviously they kept in a secure, secret location since a heart removed is incredibly vulnerable to a shaft of wood being shoved in it by an enemy . . . or, get this: *remove their own heart and lung for the awakening of their Usher.*

(This is where our translation gets a bit sloppy, okay, that's not the only place hahahahaha hahahaha haha: it's unclear as to whether the heart and lung must come from someone of that Elder's lineage.)

Now, it seems like that wouldn't work, right? Cutting out your heart and lung and giving it to someone else . . . except that removing one's heart and lung does nothing to one of the Everlasting.

So that thrall would be walking around without a heart or lung and their Usher, the Elder, would have inside *them* that thrall's heart and lung which, of course, gives the Elder a sort of second life—since someone piercing this heart would actually cause the thrall whose heart it is to turn to ash. And the Elder, being awake, stays awake, their heart and lung safely wherever they hid them.

[Transcriptionist Note: Evelyn: Doesn't removing the heart and lung drop that thrall into the Slumber? Or does removing the heart and lung without also performing the ritual allow them, as you posit, to walk around without a heart or lung . . . Go ahead and clarify in the transcription or send me a note and I will amend it.]

This also potentially explains accounts of so-called "Elders so powerful they could walk in the sun"—*they wore someone else's heart.* They didn't turn to ash because the thrall whose heart it is turned to ash. I'm not entirely sure that this explains away testament about these day-walking

Elders, since *I'm* not about to take my heart out and step into the sun to see if I don't turn to ash . . . and it's probably just a story meant to scare younger Everlasting anyway . . . but think of it, Nikolai. How terrifying?

Wait. If it was true why wouldn't we all take out our heart and hide it somewhere and walk around whenever we wanted like gods? Is the mere suggestion that it might not be grounds enough to not even try? Want to test it? Hahahahaha hahahaha-haha [incoherent]. But seriously, I bet with more research we could figure out a way to combine this ritual with a few others in the archives to allow for at least *some* daywalking by a strong enough Everlasting.

Or I'm having delusions of grandeur because how many before me have foolishly, arrogantly thought the same thing?

Some final notes here . . . the process of removing the heart and lung seems quite literal, surgical—a carving-out of these two organs which, of course, can't be pleasant. But the "putting back" of the heart and lung—their own or that of a thrall—seems to be an entirely mystical process requiring no cutting, carving, slicing, or dicing hahahaha [incoherent].

Have you ever carved a pumpkin, Nikolai? [Incoherent.]

Now

HUNTER HEARS THE CLATTER OF THE FLIMSY METAL tray meeting stone floor as an apple rolls a foot farther inside. A can of soda rolls after, in an arc ending underneath the hung lantern. With a screw from the shelving, Hunter scratches a line into the stone of the wall by the water jugs where two different systems of tallies will mark an estimated passage of time: meals and days, the latter based on the former.

Every fourth tally above is to be circled and earns a tallied "day" below. Breakfast, lunch, dinner, and a nighttime meal. He reasons that he'll still likely be served four meals a day and probably at roughly the same times as before, as his hunger between them hasn't changed considerably and the meals themselves have stayed familiar, if pared back: smaller portions, simpler preparation, sometimes stale remnants of an earlier meal—but nothing inedible. Just a noticeable difference in care and attention; he's alive, even if his stomach grumbles a little while before another tray of food appears.

They're still feeding you. Why?

A sandwich and soda now means it's probably lunchtime, maybe nighttime. The nighttime meal was always a bit random, but usually more like a lunch than a full-on dinner. He thought he would hover at the gap in the bottom of the door until someone brought his food, get a glimpse up the stairs as they opened the door to see if light shone through so he could get an idea of what time it might be—at least whether it was daytime or night—but the door at the top of the stairs doesn't seem to lead outside, at least not directly enough to allow light to filter through.

Still, the first meal he got down here was breakfast—eggs, buttered toast and jam, bacon, and a thermos of hot coffee. Based on the timing of their failed escape, he might not have been deprived a meal as punishment. Or they withheld a full cycle of meals, his hunger overridden by his being unconscious. No way to account for that missing time unfortunately.

From what he can tell, two different people bring his meals. The first wears work boots, their footfalls punctuated with the occasional masculine grunt heard before Hunter can see them, lets the tray clatter, often spilling some of the contents, like the apple Hunter picks up and dusts off on his shirt now.

The other walks more softly, either considerably smaller of stature or taking care to be quiet, and reaches in to set the tray down as carefully as a two-inch gap at the floor will allow, somehow managing to never reach far enough in for Hunter to see whether they wear any jewelry, or what pallor their skin might be. He almost never hears this person until the tray is deposited, like now, and only just catches a glimpse of them darting up the stairs, jeans and skate shoes. *A kid?*

You're clever, he laughs to himself, biting into the apple as he takes his tray to a low seat he's built of the bottom shelf of one of the shelving units, some extra bedding as padding, the center shelf removed to give his head some clearance. His throne.

You're clever, but you're soft.

His jaw drops, a mass of half-chewed apple plopping onto his shirt.

You're soft. Even for a mortal, you're soft—but you're not simple. This is the first time you've ever had to survive and you're doing a pretty poor job of it.

He stands, chucking the apple at the opposite wall. It connects with a wet thud, echoed when it hits the floor.

"Poor? I inventoried supplies. I took apart some

of the shelves for parts. I'm tallying meals to determine days. I'm rationing water. I have a warm, dry place to sleep," he mutters to no one, pacing. "Food. Water. Shelter. Done and done and *done*."

But he knows he's still alive by the grace of his captors. These thoughts have been creeping in. Sometimes they're in his voice but sometimes not. How long until the mind starts inventing the other half of the conversation?

This many days it would seem. He laughs again, scooping the apple off the floor and wiping it on his shirt before taking another bite. The dirt clinging to the meat of it doesn't bother him, like the dirt soiling his bedding, his clothes, his skin, his hair. Dirt's become as much of him as his flesh, a sort of second flesh.

"Even for a mortal. Even for a mortal. I am a mortal. I am *immortal*," he growls in a deep, horror-movie monster voice before bursting into laughter. "Now say *that* three times fast," he challenges no one and no one responds.

Now

TEMPERANCE LIGHTS THE CHARRED WICKS OF THE three black pillar candles Evelyn gave her, arranged in a triangle on a vintage mirrored tray, each flame reflected in the glass of the window overlooking the sprawling gardens of her estate. Carved on each are symbols she doesn't understand but she doesn't need to, needs only to sit on the thick ivory cushion of the window seat and gaze into the reflection in the glass—never the mirror and never the flames directly, not once they've been lit and the herbs Evelyn gave her to sprinkle over them start burning.

Tendrils of smoke curl upwards and she inhales deeply, cedar and lilac overpowered by anise. A thick silver wrap bracelet snakes up her wrist, adorned with stones the names of which escape her and in colors she didn't even know existed, each Evelyn catalogued to her at length. She explained to Temperance that traveling astrally might be easier but the idea of it—of her spirit-self or her soul (do Everlasting even have souls?) or her essence leaving her body to find her target frightened her. No, leave that to the witch.

Still, Evelyn warned her this method of connection, telepathy, could be taxing depending on the distance and whether her subject would resist her efforts, if they were cognizant of them at all. She explained to Temperance that she did her best to minimize barriers between her and her intended: the candles, the symbols, the herbs, the mirror, the window, the bracelet, probably even things Temperance didn't know about and would rather *not* know about—but the trinkets Evelyn had forged for her informants were intended for scrying, not communication.

A soft ringing in her ears and her hand attached to the wrist that wears the bracelet twitches as if with a jolt of electricity—not painful, but not pleasant, startling, foreign, as when nerves reattach in a surgical scar. She dare not look down, afraid what might happen if she catches her own reflection in the mirror, though for all she knows it's superstition or the witch messing with her, obscuring the truth so Temperance relies on her for future magical transactions. Phantom breath catches in her throat as she feels the window seat sway beneath her like a porch swing on a warm day except here no breeze ruffles her hair, just smoke tendriling and creating a haze between her and her reflection in the dim light. Her hand twitches again, this time causing her to recoil it to her chest in surprise, her other hand grabbing at the first protectively.

That's when she sees the faint outline of someone else where her reflection once danced in the flickering candlelight, as if carved from the smoke itself. In the next second, both she and the other exist in the glass, obscured somewhat by the thick, sweet smoke.

"Temperance? Is that you? What's going on? How did you get in?" She hears the words but the voice is all wrong or not at all. In her head?

"I'm not there. Can you hear me? Are you somewhere I can speak freely?"

"Well, you're speaking in my mind, so yeah— what's up, love?"

She reaches a hand up and towards the reflection, slowly stretching out her arm so she's almost touching it. Beyond the smoke outline of her informant she sees the cast of the moon like a third eye in the center of the smoke-figure's forehead. The heat of the candles and the cool of the night on the glass cause a thin layer of condensation to form, rendering the moon a smudgy blob of glow.

"New information has been uncovered about the ritual they're using to awaken Ismae the Bloody.

The translation was wrong." She cocks her head to the side, studying the shape. "The blood of those kids was never going to awaken her—a woman named Delilah is the key."

"We've met."

"You have?"

"Sure. She and this other woman—a redhead that controls the shadows—killed Johnny. Mostly the other woman since it was the shadows that swallowed him up or something, but Lydia is *livid*. Gunning for revenge, in true Lydia fashion."

Temperance sighs. She picks up on the affection in the figure's voice and she'd be lying if she said she didn't also feel some kinship with her estranged Childe. What she saw in Lydia before she Ushered her never faded—if anything, when she left the Keepers for the Praedari, Temperance saw in her eyes exactly what led her to her in the first place. She could have manipulated her, called upon the Gifts of their Blood to persuade her to stay, but Temperance knew it would be in vain. She often found herself wondering if the Becoming may have heightened those qualities in her, just as it had her eidetic memory.

"They need one of her lineage to awaken her," Temperance explains.

"I thought the kids were the mortals of her lineage—the ones that were easiest to find, anyway. God knows an Everlasting as old as Ismae could probably claim a continent."

Temperance says, "Delilah is the Grandchilde of Ismae the Bloody."

"She still has descendants among the Everlasting?" A long, low whistle slices through Temperance's mind as she winces, followed by a familiar chuckle. "And he needs *her* blood? That's a fight I wouldn't sign on for. Scrappy, that one, and tough." Though her informant is not here to see her, she shakes her head *no* before catching herself and to her surprise the voice speaks again in answer:

"No? Then what?"

"Her heart and her lung." She presses her palm

to the glass of the window, inhaling sharply in anticipation of something that doesn't come. Just cool of glass against the cool of her dead palm, the sensations canceling one another out save for the head radiating upward from the flickering candles. She frowns. "Your question tells me that at least *you* didn't know of her connection to Ismae. Did you know Ismae Ushered Ezekiel Winter?"

"Not at all. The Praedari aren't big on record-keeping and her Ushering a prominent Keeper would weaken their claim that she's their mother, the first Praedari." The figure pauses a beat, then adds, "I mean—sorry. I know that Lydia . . . Anyway, does Victor know about Delilah yet?" She feels the familiar squirm of someone trying hard not to offend, even through the magics handed to her by Evelyn. No wonder she cautioned her against making this a habit. Temperance shrugs in answer, another gesture she's not sure the voice can see but they answer their own question nonetheless: "You need me to make sure he does *if* he doesn't already. Won't that put her in danger?"

"Well, he would still have to *find* her. None of us can, it seems," she says with a sigh.

"Temperance, Delilah is *here*. She arrived the first night of the Howling and hasn't left. She and Victor seem quite familiar. At least, he seems familiar with her. She seems a bit blindsided by all of it. Mina almost had her Hunted—would've, too, if Victor hadn't barged in."

"And?"

"And then he had Liam and Mina greet the sun as punishment."

Temperance pauses to frown, the line of her mouth turning down in her reflection on the window glass, juxtaposed against the smoke-figure she speaks with. Only now does she realize this reflection does not bear the curse of the Everlasting. She sees herself as others see her, not as she is. She wonders if the mirror Evelyn cautioned her against looking into tonight would show her this same self, or if it holds her future self, that decay unto the ash of her Final Moment. Maybe it holds her Final Moment, or the truth of it. The oldest punishment, the sun—elegant, beautiful in its simplicity, almost poetic. Where the Praedari might not care much for Keeper lineages, the Council of Keepers know well the few more notable lineages among the Praedari, Liam and Mina's included. But whatever happened to their sister?

"Delilah knew the relative danger going into this, just as you did," she starts. "But this has the potential to escalate quickly, so we must tread carefully."

"Lydia was assigned to be her security, though that hasn't come about yet. I could press Victor about that when I deliver the news. That way I can keep an eye on her, too. There have been rumblings here among the others—they don't trust her and they don't trust him trusting her. And while Liam and Mina weren't well-liked, no one is pleased with Victor's decision to make an example of them for her sake."

"That could work. She has a trinket like yours, less permanent, of course—but I fear she's lost it, foolish girl. Who receives a gift and does not open it? I need you to nudge her, without giving up your cover. If she has it—"

"She does! I got a hold of her bag when Liam and Mina were dragged off. The box was in there—the same box you gave me mine in, navy velvet. There was a tear in the lining of her bag that I slipped it into. It's definitely not well-hidden, but she had enough junk in there that someone might not find it unless they were looking for it. I gave it to Victor and I think he returned it to her. I stole her copy of *We Have Always Lived in the Castle*, though, just in case. I can use it as an excuse to drop by her quarters."

"No, I don't want you putting yourself at risk like that. You've been there since the beginning. I'm interested in the dissent you mentioned—if that escalates, it endangers you both, but it might also be a useful distraction. Nudge her, but not directly."

"Got it."

"And then make sure Victor gets the information about the ritual."

With that, she uses her reflection in the mirror to guide her hand above one of the lit candles, its heat warming her palm a moment before she brings it down to smother the flame. She winces at the hot-sharp, the smell of burnt flesh mingling with the herbal smoke. A familiar sensation rises in her, the swelling of an ocean wave as it breaks surface but she swallows down that part of her as she has for centuries, as she will continue to for as long as she rises each night.

She raises her palm again and extinguishes the second burning candle in the same manner, then the third, her reflection in the window glass and the heat itself as guide. She dare not look down, even carefully, for fear of a wayward glance at her true self in the calm surface of the mirror, though she cannot lie to herself: some part of her not her, or some part of her more her than she's allowed herself to be in a long time, urges her from some depth to just sneak a peek, what could it hurt?

The cedar-lilac-anise smoke dissipates and where once the cloying of the sweet smoke now the smell of burnt flesh. She stands and turns from the makeshift altar of the window seat, careful not to catch her reflection in the mirror as Evelyn warned her against. She clutches her burnt palm to her chest, eyeing the small tin of salve Evelyn gave her.

A kindness, it would seem: but the witch always exacts a price.

Now

"WHAT WERE YOU GUYS THINKING?!"

The whoosh of the doors opening and shutting causes her to turn in her sleep, but it's an uncharacteristically shrill Lydia jumping on her that jolts Kiley awake. Clutched in her hand is a pen which she holds like a knife as she stabs blindly in the dark at the disturbance. Her journal lay open next to her, clattering as she knocks it to the floor in her blind self-defense.

"Seriously?!" Lydia continues in a loud whisper, shoving Kiley into wakefulness. "Whatever you did you *really* ticked off Victor. Give me that," she hisses, grabbing Kiley's pen from her hand and tossing it onto her nightstand. "Wake up. Talk."

"We're *human. We* sleep at night," Kiley mumbles, swinging a pillow which connects with her arm with a dull thud. "Why're you here? Why do you care?"

Lydia shrugs. "Well, I like *you.*" She tugs Kiley upright. "Do I need to make you some coffee or what? Why are you sleeping at night? Are you sick?"

"Because I'm human, remember?" Kiley repeats with a smirk.

"Yeah, but all the action around here's at night. Speaking of action, spill. What did you guys *do?* I'm here against orders. No one is supposed to come in or out. You've been quarantined." With that last statement she crosses her arms out in front of her like the letter X, laughing.

"Quarantines are for infectious diseases, not hostage situations," Kiley explains, sitting up.

"Hostages? No one's demanded ransom," Lydia quips. "Anyway, no one is supposed to interact with you. Victor put my pack on a different block so I had to wait until I could sneak away. He probably moved us because he knew I'd sneak away—but putting me on a different security detail meant I at least had to wait a while."

"I was wondering why we—I—hadn't seen you," Kiley remarks. She tries to keep the disappointment out of her voice. "It felt like forever," Kiley pouts.

"Yeah, well, time passes a little differently when you live forever." There's a defensiveness to her voice that Kiley can't help but notice, but it softens nearly as quickly as it came on. "I *wanted* to come, but had to wait until the heat was off. Whatever you guys did, it's put Victor on edge. The only reason he hasn't completely gone off the rails is because he's been distracted by that Keeper, Delilah."

Kiley's eyes narrow. "Why don't you ask *her* what happened?"

"Was she involved?" Lydia feigns looking surprised.

"You know she was," Kiley calls her out with a trace of a smile.

"Yeah, busted," she admits. "I overheard some others talking about it, but I didn't hear the beginning of their conversation. I really don't know what happened, or her part of things. I just know Victor didn't tie her to a tree and let sunrise claim her."

The ease with which Lydia suggests sunrise as a possible outcome for this Delilah woman leaves no doubt in Kiley's mind that it could've been. "Well, Charlie melted something in the backup generator somehow—with some chemical or something—so it didn't kick on when the main generator restarted for the night. We ran. Delilah found us."

"Wait, wait, wait. Delilah turned you guys in?" Lydia asks, trying to piece it together. "Or did she help you guys? Wait, how did Charlie get out of here to melt the generator in the first place? How do you even melt a generator?"

"We *thought* Delilah was helping us—we ran into her in the hallway after the main generator went down," Kiley explains. "Then she turned us into Victor first chance she got. And like I said, Charlie did something with a chemical or something, I don't know. The plan wasn't to literally explode it."

"Where's Hunter?" Lydia asks, gesturing to his empty bed.

"They took him." Kiley presses her lips together, willing herself not to cry despite the tears that sting her eyes whenever she thinks of him.

"They *who*?" Lydia's voice softens.

"I don't know, some guy, I'd never seen him before. Victor had him sent away," Kiley elaborates. "The woman who dragged me back here says he's as good as dead." She clenches her jaw to keep from crying. "They both had red hair."

"Liam and Mina," Lydia suggests. "And Hunter's not dead," she offers, then catches herself. "I mean, probably not. I don't want to build up false hope, but I can try to find out for sure. Some of the mortal staff was instructed to send food down to the cellar at the same times they've been sending food here and unless a staffer got into trouble, that might be him."

"I knew it!" Kiley throws her arms around Lydia. "Please. He's my friend. We *all* tried to escape, Victor just picked Hunter to make an example of."

"Well, just because he's alive . . . I wouldn't celebrate, is all I'm saying," she cautions. "And like I said, Victor's been weird lately, it's not like I can just ask him."

Kiley nods, but she can't stop her lips from tugging up into a smile. "I'm sorry! It's just the closest thing to good news I've had since they took Hunter away." Then she adds, "Hey, aren't the Keepers supposed to be the nice ones? The ones that *help* humans?"

Lydia's turn to shrug. She flops down on her side on Kiley's bed, looking too comfortable given the situation, like a friend at a slumber party ready to share secrets. She's missed her. Charlie called it Stockholm Syndrome.

"Keepers, well, that depends who you ask. Their thing is hiding, staying to the shadows so you guys don't know vampires exist. If you ask me, that's not really helping as much as deceiving."

"As opposed to openly hunting us? Or almost killing Charlie?" Kiley grumbles.

"Hey, you asked. That other pack wasn't supposed to land Charlie in the infirmary," Lydia defends.

"Wasn't it your pack that chased Hunter all over and then blew up part of a metro terminal to get to him?"

"Look, we were making a political statement and he walked away unhurt. Besides, this place will probably do more good for you humans than the Keepers ever have."

"What do you mean?" Kiley asks, cocking her head. "There's absolutely no reason you shouldn't tell me." Kiley offers. "What am *I* going to do about it?"

Lydia rolls onto her back and sighs. "You're actually right about that."

13

Now

I LINK MY ARM THROUGH VICTOR'S AS HE LEADS ME down a series of gleaming, sterile hallways. We've crossed the threshold of where my key card allows me to be several turns ago, the facility here seeming far larger inside than it appears on the outside—a trick of the architecture as we head nearly imperceptibly underground, the gradient of the slope subtle enough to go almost undetected.

I've heard Victor, Lydia, others call this "the facility" but as we delve farther, deeper, it feels almost like a hive, a secret self-contained, self-sufficient, alive. In truth, Keepers refer to cohabitating

Praedari within a territory as nests or hives, but derisively, undermining their agency and strength, likening them to nothing more than pests in need of extermination. This, though, pulses with power, with life, with purpose.

Victor doesn't speak, a sort of excitement alight in him dimming even the too-bright fluorescents overhead. He leads on with a smile, but it isn't much farther until when we're met with another set of sealed doors that could be from a sci-fi series, this time marked with a biohazard symbol that takes up the entirety of both, straddling the barely-visible seam where they meet, and outlined by black and yellow diagonally striped paint. The same paint serves as a welcome mat on the floor.

Victor steps towards a screen waiting to display biometric readouts, pressing his left thumb to it until an electronic whir and high-pitched tone of confirmation sound—then he does the same with his left index finger. He then stands straight, looking forward, eyes open as facial recognition software seems satisfied, and then a retinal scan completes and the same series of tones are heard. Then he speaks, clear and evenly: "Alpha-November-Zulu-Delta-Whiskey-Bravo-Zero-Zero-One-Zero-Three-Nine-Seven." The voice recognition software lights up with the now-familiar set of tones and then announces: *"Match for subject ANZ-DWB 0010397."*

Victor taps the screen a few more times before the same voice announces: *"Access granted for subject ANZ-DWB 0010397 and guest."*

The doors separate without the whoosh the doors to my suite sing out whenever they open or close, though their movement is similarly fluid. The silence of the doors themselves undermined by the low, steady *whomp-whomp-whomp* wail of an alarm announcing our presence. The doors open into a small chamber with another set of similarly marked doors, biohazard symbol and stripes. When we step inside, the doors behind us seal.

"This is a sterilization chamber. A mist of a

proprietary chemical compound will spray us down—it's harmless, mortal staffers breath it in multiple times a day," Victor says with a wave of his hand. "It won't ruin your clothes or anything. Stand like this on these marks." He guides me into position, my legs spread so my feet plant where outlines of feet are marked on the floor. He stands the same way on another mark next to me. Ahead of us on the wall is a silhouette indicating that we are also to put our arms out to our sides and look straight ahead, eyes closed.

Sound of mist—so fine and dry the skin can't feel it.

"Really it wouldn't even burn your eyes, but it's a precaution," he says as the sound of the mist-spray stops. "The mortals working here that are exposed to this compound daily have had remarkable health—I think our research team is ready to file for a patent and start the red tape with the FDA. I'm not quite sure what they're thinking as far as application outside the facility, but our research and medical teams here boast some of the brightest, if unconventional, minds in the field. We have to be careful about possible contamination—it's a delicate ecosystem we've built. You'll understand in a moment." He places his hand on the small of my back, urging me towards the next set of doors which open without being prompted.

Victor gestures with a wide sweep of his arm in front of us, beaming. "Welcome to Project Harvest."

A wave of dizziness. Like a shotgun burst from my heart up through my throat, the predator within me lunges towards freedom. I feel as though I am being torn through, as if this beast's claws were not also my own, her fangs not also my fangs though I feel them with my tongue before I throw my head back with a snarl. In this moment, I am two: the vessel and what's contained inside.

Four teenagers lie sleeping, tubes like IVs in each of their arms. I cannot see to what they are connected—beyond them I see only the dirt I once climbed out from and a mangled shape slumped, surrounded by a dark pool. That is not here and some part of me knows this. The vessel or what's inside?

A me that's not me walks towards the wet that I know isn't there and smells a familiar metallic tang that might be. In the mirror-like surface of the dark pool half-conjured from memory, stars appear as tiny flecks of light around my face. They flit like fireflies. My hair matted with phantom dirt and my face caked with remembered dark, nausea washes over me. That much is very *real, something spilling from the vessel that is me with the splash of wet-on-tile. The reflection swirls and changes to that of a beautiful woman, pale, sleeping like the four teenagers, but with a thick tube down her throat rather than in her arms like IVs. She feels familiar. I want to touch her. I think of Snow*

White. Then of the poison apple. Which was the vessel,
and what was inside?

    Time passes.

    Her eyes open.

    I can feel her hunger.

14

Now

AT ONCE HUNTER FINDS HIMSELF PITCHING FOR-ward, hands reaching out for wall or shelf or anything to catch himself but missing. With a hard crash he's aware of cans clattering to the floor and rolling. Then nothing. So many moments of nothing that could all be one moment, a single tick of the hand of a clock counting a second or eighty-six thousand of them.

But not quite nothing, or nothing, and then not nothing. A blurry somethingness, soft around the edges and murky in the middle, like stirring up the sludge at the bottom of a pond and watching it dissipate upwards towards the surface. He's aware that he groans, feeling the vibration of sound in his throat though the sound itself is swallowed by the nothing just beyond his lips. Or what's a groan if there's no one else to hear it?

A dark mirrored floor and four figures, each hooked up with tubes leading to bags of red and from those bags of red to one thick tube down the throat of a woman who's bound at the wrists and ankles, eyes closed. Asleep? Hunter smells blood. Blood and apple, chewed-up apple he dropped on his shirt earlier.

Ah, yes. There I am. And there you are. The same voice that startled the apple from his mouth.

"I'm not there."

Look closer, and he does, or he finds that he does, more an effect of the command than of his own agency.

Logan, Charlie, Kiley, himself, and now he notices where a fifth would have lain, each in a bed, Spartan in its simplicity: raw wood, single thin mattress. He looks down, an intricate grid of geometric shapes outlined between the four of them and the empty bed in the center, each line a depression in the mirrored surface of the floor. The center: a woman with the thick tube down her throat, elevated above the rest on a cement block, as if an offering on an altar to something horrific unnamed, the tubes from each of the four of them a crimson web leading to her own. Where once her wrists and ankles were bound, now they are chained.

I'm not the offering.

Hunter lies on his back on the dirty floor, a couple drops of blood tickling a trail from his nostril to his upper lip, leaving a red smear when he wipes it.

"We are," he states simply. "But . . . who are you?"

I am the Mother.

15

Now

ARMS ENCIRCLE ME AND WHERE I WAS ONCE A LIMP rag doll now I wriggle and writhe and strain against the body to which they're connected, jutting out my hip in an attempt to knock them off balance. Smells like wild. I manage to turn halfway around, my jaw snapping, catching nothing between my teeth. Someone speaks, but words slosh into and out of my ears, drowned out by my own snarls. I spin face-to-face with the one who restrains me.

He smells like the closest thing I have to memory, like pine and wildflowers and sweat. My predator within recoils—no, she doesn't recoil, coils, ribboning back, retreating into a part of me I haven't felt for a long time except for phantom twinges, wrapping herself snakelike around my dead heart. Why doesn't she attack? My torso pressed against his, his arms still encircling me—more of an embrace now than restraint, except my arms are pinned between us.

He pulls me tighter against him, bending his neck so his head dips into the crook of my neck, hovering without touching just a moment before his lips plant a kiss, then another and another. His fangs slide forward, their cool hardness resting on my skin. Threat or promise? I press my own fangs into the soft flesh of his neck, enough pressure to make small divots but not puncture, not draw blood.

With a growl I shove myself free of his embrace, stumbling backwards myself as I don't anticipate the heaviness of his stance, a trick of his Blood or a symptom of my fugue state. I crash to the floor, my head knocking back into a wall.

"Delilah!" I blink a few times, realizing Victor has followed me to the floor, kneeling and concerned—not for the impact, as harmless as a mosquito bite despite the gash on my scalp, but for awakening the feral thing within me. "I'm sorry," he says. "I should've warned you. I didn't think you'd react quite like this."

"How did you *expect* me to react?!" Though even *I'm* not sure what I would call the reaction I just had, in one moment ready to kill and the next kiss.

"Disgust or fear, maybe, at first. Curiosity."

As Victor speaks I stare past him at a vast network of clear tubes, each pumping red from somewhere to somewhere else like veins. "Each" if any were discernible from the tangle, but instead a thick web between rows and rows of clear cylindrical containers, many too far to make out the shape contained within.

The rows nearest us, though—despite the

pungent citrus and bleach of disinfectant in the recycled air, I have no doubt what energy buzzes in this hive, what pushes through this web from the cylinders with their gelatinous vellum of thick wet buoying bodies within, some with hair splayed like a crown around their heads, suspended. A panel of biometric readouts on each, monitors and lights and numbers illuminated: heart rate, pulse, glucose and oxygen levels, various temperature readouts.

" . . . wonderment. It's a marvel of medical progress and the result of decades of research," he continues explaining, though I've missed part of it.

"This is a blood farm."

"Put in crude terms, yes, a blood farm," he says, offering a hand to help me up from the floor. "But Project Harvest is so much more. Come, let me walk you around."

His hand on the small of my back, he guides me along a clearly-marked walkway edged in the black-and-yellow diagonal stripes bidding us caution in both of the doorways securing this place from the prying eyes of the rest of the facility. Every few feet there is a reminder to keep to the walkway and not touch the tanks or tubework.

"Meet the donors," he smiles, bidding I follow him off the walkway and step with him towards one of the tanks. Suspended inside is a woman with IVs taped to both of her forearms with white medical tape and a tube down her throat. She appears unharmed, her skin a healthy glow, the rise-fall of her chest steady, likely assisted by the tube.

"How is she not breathing in the liquid?" I ask from a foot behind him, just beyond the edge of the walkway, afraid to come closer.

"It's much firmer than it appears, more like a hardening gelatin—and you can't see it, but there's actually a sort of thin bubble or layer of air around her, so the substance never actually touches her. Though it could, it's harmless. And all necessary nutrients and hydration are provided by the IV. Each pod—we call them *tanks*—is a self-sustaining

ecosystem attuned to the specific dietary and medical needs of the donor."

"Donor? Each of these people . . . volunteered?"
By my estimate there's at least a few hundred—
maybe a thousand tanks, though it's difficult to see
if each is active.

"They are donating their time and their blood,
yes. In exchange, they are paid—each is contracted
for a set amount of time, currently not exceeding
three months—and while they are in our care any
medical conditions they have are treated to the best
of our ability, and cured if it's possible. In the cases
of those donors with currently incurable life-threat-
ening illnesses, tissue may be sampled so our
medical team can continue researching a cure, but
it's all in the waiver they sign during orientation. In
the case that something in research looks promising,
those donors afflicted with that condition will be
given the option to enter into a study at the end of
their donor contract. None of this is without risk,
of course," he explains. "But the potential here,

Delilah! AIDS, cancer, fibromyalgia, birth defects—we never take on pregnant donors, of course, but by studying the body like we can here . . . no other research facility, public, private or government, matches the potential of what you see here."

I've stepped back onto the walkway by the end of his speech, hands clasped at my breast for fear of accidentally touching something I shouldn't.

"Now you understand why we were so frantic to get the power back on when that generator failed. This part of the facility has other fail-safes in place, of course, but it was a wake-up call for us."

He leads us farther into the huge room, the walkway a loop.

"But . . . why? Why?"

"You weren't wrong, Delilah—it *is* a blood farm. We harvest and store blood from donors to sustain ourselves—the medical research, while important and cutting-edge, fell into our laps years ago when I hired our lead physician and medical researcher, Dr. Larkin."

"Some Keepers use the services of mortal blood banks to minimize the need to hunt—but hunting is sacred to the Praedari. If you can sustain a population on this and eliminate the need to hunt—"

"—why would this facility be pioneered by the Praedari?" He finishes my question.

I nod.

"It's politics, Delilah. Yes, Project Harvest challenges one of the most steadfast principles held by the Praedari: the right and need to hunt. But you know what else Project Harvest does? Scares the Keepers. After centuries of silence we matter again. That noise, the chaos out *there*—that matters more to the sect right now than tradition. So, at the rallies and when our leadership checks in I pay lip service, I say the right things. They get a rise out of your Elders and I get Project Harvest."

Victor continues. "Mortal politicians play the game. Your Elders play the game. Your Usher, Delilah, we all knew who he was, what he was after, the sort of secrets he kept—and we all know it wasn't the Praedari that killed him—but it's a *game*. By not denying it, our silence made enough noise to start a war.

"While our leadership and your Elders scheme and plot and ally and double-cross—while they hold secret meetings and argue the same drawn-out arguments they have for centuries—Project Harvest becomes an ideal the youth of both sects can embrace and champion. As soon as you ended up on our doorstep, I wanted you to see this for yourself. I wanted you to understand what this could mean for *all* of us. I wanted the chance to convince you of the good we're doing here.

"Do you believe that Project Harvest is immoral, Delilah?"

"We hide in the shadows . . . " I say, part of the Oath of the Keepers conjured from deep within me.

"No. Not your faction, not what the Elders handed down as law. Delilah, do *you* believe Project Harvest is immoral? Evil? Wrong? And do you believe that as guardians of humanity the Keepers have succeeded?"

He pauses, looking into my eyes. I can't help but focus on his lips as they move—lips I've both known and forgotten, lips I've since felt on my own, lips I can't wait to meet again. A shiver starts at the top of my head and sinks down my spine, and I'm suddenly quite aware that I'm staring.

"We are prepared to defend ourselves, and the hundreds of helpless donors who cannot defend themselves." His voice softens. "And I—I'm prepared to defend *you*."

Now

"Y**OU'RE THE MOTHER? OF WHO?**" H**UNTER PULLS** himself up to sitting, scooting back against the cement vault in the center of his cell. He wipes his nose but the bleeding has stopped, now crumbles of blood where it bled. "Where are you, anyway? How are you in my head?"

So many questions but none of them the right one. I'm here. *With you.*

"In my heart?" he scoffs, putting a hand to his chest and finding comfort in the beating there. He rests his head back against the cool cement, looking up at the ceiling. "And if I just believe—"

—No, you dolt. The voice interrupts as a wave of sound, causing him to wince at her—her?—volume. *I'm here. With you. I can hear your heart reverberate through the cement and rebar of this, my burial vault.*

Hunter's head snaps forward and he scrambles a few feet from the cement structure, the rough of the floor rubbing his knees through his jeans and digging into his palms, but he does not notice. He flips himself onto his butt again when he runs into the metal shelving, out of space to put between him and whatever is in the box.

"You—you what?!"

And there, faint again, but your breathing quickened. You're afraid. I can smell it. Do you know what fear smells like, Hunter? I suppose it's different for everyone—yours reminds me of petrichor and coffee. Or maybe it's earthworms splayed open on sidewalks after the rain and coffee. Fear is always a pungent scent. When you're as old as I, you find ways to dull it so it doesn't overwhelm you. You're afraid, but you needn't be. You're the safest that you've been here since they brought you to this place. None of them want to visit me and, thus, they shall leave you alone. Until they do not, of course.

"No, no, no, no. No." He shakes his head so hard a familiar pang shoots up his neck and he winces, the burning sensation spreading from the point of tension and radiating up and down, outward from that spot. He's been so long without a proper bed that, well, he's essentially talking to his bed. He laughs. "No. I'm alone here. I'm talking to myself. I'm talking to a cement slab. I'm talking to my bed."

Yes, I thought that an odd choice but I suppose I'm not sure what it looks like in this cellar, just that we are in one and sometimes you allow me glimpses. I find it curious that you'd rather be alone and crazy than consider that I could be real, even though my being real should come as a comfort?

"If you're real—what are you? How are you living in a box with no air? I mean." He cranes his neck, reassessing whether the structure might be airtight. He shakes his head. "I don't think it's necessarily airtight, but there's no way you're getting much oxygen."

I'm not. Inside this vault is my coffin and inside my coffin is me. I'm a vampire. That much should be obvious, should it not?

He looks around for something to use as a weapon; his eyes falling on a bracket from a shelving unit he took apart. One hand, one knee. The other hand, the other knee. He crawls to the bracket and takes it up slowly.

You needn't slink. I can hear that you've moved.

"If you're a vampire, why are you being kept down here? Are you one of them, a Praedari? A Keeper? Are you a prisoner? *Why* are you a prisoner?" He shudders at this last question: what could she have done that was so terrible as to earn imprisonment by these bloodsucking monsters? Even when Victor captured that Delilah woman, from the rival faction, he treated her like a welcome guest. Even *he* was treated kindly upon arrival until they all decided to try to escape. And even now, he's alive, fed, warm enough.

It was foolish of you all. You were safe—he wasn't lying, he thought they needed your blood, but you could have walked away alive. Now you're lucky you're down here with me, for I know what is coming. Do you really want to know who I am?

"Yes," he answers, not missing a beat.

17

Now

MORGEAUX PACES AT THE COUNTER OF A DINER IN a dingy truck stop, TVs blaring some conservative news channel. Her burger and fries are cold, a few bites missing, soda half-finished. The waitress, hair teased big and lips too red and painted on crookedly, looks at her and reaches for the plastic tumbler that reminds Morgeaux of her school cafeteria. She just nods and the woman vanishes behind a partition, staring at her through the greenish dimpled glass.

Quinn sits on a torn red vinyl stool, the tan foam inside peeking through, watching the girl. She wears her red hair in her usual messy braids, trading in her usual tunic and shield and opting tonight for more modern dress—a pair of black leggings and a black jersey tunic with crisscrossed straps at the chest, black Doc Martens.

"You don't have to do this, you know? We can go back to the safehouse before your memory of it fades," Quinn says, but the girl shakes her head in response.

"Here you go, darlin'" the waitress purrs as she sets the glass down to the ring of wet it left behind before she took it for a refill. "She's right, ya know. Whatever you're trying to escape—drugs, an ex, the past—it's always easier with a lock between you and it."

"Nah. I'm tired of running."

The waitress shrugs and all three women focus on the television on the back wall as a familiar phrase hangs heavy in the air: breaking news.

"Breaking news: the President, rumored to be pressured by National Security Council, to declare a State of Emergency due to the recent threats to key government officials." The voice drops to a loud whisper as the din in the press conference room quiets. "We are live at the White House now."

"A State of Emergency is hereby declared in the continental United States, Alaska, Hawaii, and its outlying territories and military bases, effective immediately.

"This State of Emergency has been declared due to civil unrest and widespread acts of domestic terrorism. It is the hope of the Department of Defense and all relevant government agencies that other countries' leadership will follow suit in an effort to protect not only their own citizens, but American citizens abroad. Only by coming together in this time of international crisis may good prevail.

"This State of Emergency will remain in effect until rescinded by a subsequent order.

"As the President of the United States of America, I hereby exercise the authority given to me by the People, for the People, to preserve the public safety and hereby render all required and available assistance vital to the security, well-being, and health of the citizens of the United States of America.

"I hereby direct all departments and agencies of the government of the United States of America to take whatever steps necessary to protect life and property, public infrastructure, and provide emergency assistance as deemed necessary.

"Furthermore, this State of Emergency includes a declaration of Martial Law, effective tomorrow evening at dusk. Curfew shall be sunset in the local time zone, in effect until dawn of the same. There will be a comprehensive guide to these times on the White House webpage under the National Security link, as well as broadcast by all United States-based news channels twenty-four-seven.

"It is likewise the hope of the National Security Council that airports, cellular networks, and social media sites will also make this information readily available. All civilians are to adhere to this without exception. Failure to do so may result in fines, imprisonment, or execution.

"Martial Law will remain in effect until rescinded by a subsequent order. Thank you."

The reporter speaks once again as the room erupts in a cacophony of press questions, all decorum lost in the fray. "You heard it here first," she half-shouts into her microphone. "The President of the United States of America minces no words in his inclusion of Martial Law in his and the National Security Council's joint declaration of a State of Emergency. We turn now to—"

The waitress leans on the coffee-stained Formica counter and continues to stare up at the broadcast, her raptor-like bright pink nails now hidden as her fingers curl underneath the edge of the counter. Quinn turns from the screen to face Morgeaux again.

"Are you sure about this?" she asks in a low whisper, dodging the previously prying ears of the waitress.

"I need to meet them. If we're a part of why all this started, maybe we can be a part of how it ends."

Headlights beam in through the diner window. A truck idles.

"I can't stop you, but I can give you this. Memory of the safehouse will fade when you strike out on your own—but this will always bring you somewhere safe," she explains, handing Morgeaux an antique pocket compass with an eight-pronged symbol in place of the traditional compass rose, simple in its linework. "*Safe* may change in meaning depending what storm you weather, but vegvisir will make sure you're never lost, even when the way is not known."

Morgeaux takes the compass and slips it into her pocket before embracing Quinn in a quick hug.

"Well met, Morgeaux."

She merely gives Quinn a nod before heading out of the truck stop diner into the night, towards the truck with its headlights illuminating their goodbye. She eyes the blonde girl, the Charlie of

Charlie and Logan, in the driver's seat whose gaze is just as intense. Beside the girl, now moving over to make room for her on the bench seat of the truck, Logan. Morgeaux goes to Charlie's open window.

"This is the truck you stole from them?"

Charlie nods.

"Come on. They'll know to look for it. Quinn told me to take hers. She'll travel through Asgard home."

"Asgard?" Charlie maintains her grip on the steering wheel, making no move to shift into park, much less turn off the truck. Morgeaux notices the gas light illuminated on the dash as Logan climbs out of the truck, slamming the door.

"Look, I've got a full tank of gas and a car they won't be looking for. If you wanna follow in this thing you've got probably what? Twenty miles in this clunker? Fifty miles if you're lucky. Less if that's been lit up long. You want to gas up while we're here?"

"We don't have money," Logan chimes in as he

comes around the truck. "Unless you're gonna gas and dash, Charlie?"

She glares at him, then shifts to park and turns off the truck, clicking off the headlights. Logan reaches for Morgeaux's hand and closes it in both of his in a firm-yet-familiar handshake as Charlie climbs from the truck.

"So you're Morgeaux." He smiles. "We've been calling you 'The One Who Got Away.' This is Charlie—The One Who Almost Died."

"I guess now we're all The One Who Got Away," Morgeaux replies with a smile. She reaches for Charlie's hand as she slams the driver's side door shut. Charlie shakes it roughly, her gaze still unflinching as she studies the new girl. "You're . . . intense, huh?" she asks, raising an eyebrow at her before looking to Logan for help diffusing the tension.

"We've been through a lot," he shrugs.

"Yeah. We have. *Together.* And somehow you got away from all of it unscathed?" Charlie challenges.

"Don't assume you know what I've been through," Morgeaux replies coolly, pulling her hand away. "Quinn and Delilah are the only reason I got away."

It's then that Charlie notices the gun tucked in the small of the girl's back as her shirt lifts an inch with her sudden movement. She notices, too, the imprint of something circular in her left front jeans pocket, the tip of something protruding from the top of her boot just barely.

"Yes, I'm packing. Useless against vampires, mostly, but old habits die hard."

Charlie's expression softens at this. "We've got some stuff in the truck we'll bring. Not ideal, but should be more effective. Some stakes we carved from furniture, a Swiss Army knife so we can carve more."

Morgeaux purses her lips in a smirk and leans down, pulling the something out of her tall boot: part of a pool cue, sharpened, the shaft of which is still polished and gleaming.

"Maybe we can upgrade you guys. It's not hard to steal these. You guys hear the President's address?"

"We did, on the radio," Logan offers. "So . . . things haven't been going well out here? We've been cut off since our capture."

Charlie looks beyond both of them to the far side of the truck stop, the faint light of what's probably headlights catching her attention before she hears the sound of tires on pavement, then the muffled laughter and music.

"Not at all. We should probably get out of here, speaking of. It's us, a cashier, and that waitress," Morgeaux adds, her eyes following Charlie's. "And that waitress is probably about half-finished with that tabloid she's been flipping through since I got here."

As if on cue, a set of headlights slices the darkness. An SUV rounds the building and grinds to a stop in front of the truck stop, taking up the better part of two spaces and nearly hitting a bright yellow cement pillar, the bumping of loud bass and laughter audible from inside.

Morgeaux turns and stands facing the SUV with Charlie, her hands hovering near her back pockets, her back to Logan as she's just a couple steps in front of him. She gestures with a hooked finger for him to step closer to her, then casually sweeps her shirt out of the way of the gun tucked in the waist of her jeans. He steps in next to her, his hand still behind her back, wrapped around the grip of her handgun, appearing from the front as if he rests it possessively on the small of her back.

A man and a woman hop out of the front seats of the SUV, still laughing about something. Though the back windows are tinted, Charlie can see they are alone. She coughs twice, looking at Morgeaux who, having noticed the direction of Charlie's gaze, gives a little nod.

"Just two or more?" she asks quietly.

"Just."

The man and the woman step around their vehicle.

"You kids shouldn't be out here. Did you hear the President's address? Curfew starts tomorrow."

"Yeah, we heard," Logan calls out. "Thanks for your concern. We were just leaving."

It all happens in near-simultaneity: The two shrug and head inside the truck stop. Logan's grip on Morgeaux's gun loosens and he takes a step away from her with an audible sigh. That's when Charlie hears the crunch of footsteps rounding the front of their truck. She whirls around, grabbing Morgeaux's gun from the waistband of her jeans and tossing Logan the stake she had tucked in her hoodie. It clatters to his feet as a woman's voice causes him and Morgeaux to join Charlie in facing the new arrivals, two men and a woman.

"Hear that? They were just leaving," she teases, pounding a fist on the hood of the truck, denting it.

"And armed to the teeth!" the man adds. "That one's got a gun. How suspicious."

Charlie raises the handgun level with his chest, stance steady. Logan stoops to grab the stake at his feet, his eyes not leaving the second man. Morgeaux stands as still as stone, eyes fixed on the woman.

"I don't miss," Charlie challenges in an effort to coax a reaction.

"I'll give you one shot, sweetheart. But you only get the one." He speaks as if to a child who's begging for a piece of candy, eyes wide, overwhelmed by choosing just one from the rows of brightly wrapped treats.

"I wouldn't do it if I was you," someone says as they come around the back of the truck. "He's magic!" The voice comes from a little boy, about ten years old if they had to guess. He punctuates his statement with wiggling jazz fingers and a giggle.

Charlie can't help but take her eyes off the man her gun is trained on for just a second, distracted by the child who remains at the end of the truck bed.

"Not breathing," she announces focusing again on the man and squeezing the trigger.

What Charlie sees next she's not ready for: the widening of eyes in slow motion as he erupts in a puff of ash, his surprise mirrored in her features and the features of his companions and, she'd guess, her own. The little boy shrieks and cowers back behind the truck.

The woman lunges for Charlie but Morgeaux steps into her path to intercept her, the end of a sharpened pool cue raised. It glances off the woman's coat as the two fall to a grapple on the pavement, Morgeaux maintaining a hold on the makeshift stake, for now.

The woman triggers a chain reaction as the other man rushes for Logan who braces for impact, crouching slightly as if in a football drill, transferring his center of gravity lower so he's not as easily taken off-balance. The man crashes into him as Logan raises the stake Charlie tossed him, using his own weight and advantageous posture to thrust and drive it into the man's chest. For a millisecond he's worried he missed the heart, but as he forces the stake deeper the man's cries are cut short and Logan finds himself covered in the ash of his remains.

Charlie tries to find an opening to shoot the woman that doesn't compromise Morgeaux's safety, but the other girl doesn't make it easy on her, pivoting to keep the woman from pinning her with her superior strength and clutching the stake in one hand as best she's able. Flailing, Charlie finally reaches to her side and scoops up a handful of sand and fine rock, using her hip to knock the woman just slightly off-balance as she heaves the debris into the woman's face with desired effect. As the woman screeches and wipes at her face instead of putting space between her and Morgeaux, the girl grips the stake in both hands and drives it forward into the woman's chest.

A powerful force from behind knocks Charlie to the ground, the gun sent sprawling across the pavement. On her stomach, she can't see who or what pins her. A hand grabs her hair and yanks her head back and in an instant something sharp presses to her throat, puncturing that delicate flesh before tearing.

Gunfire—three shots—and the hand in her hair lets go, her face hitting the pavement as she feels a warm spurt of blood, her own by the smell of it. She rolls onto her back to see Morgeaux with the gun trained on her or, rather, above her at what had her pinned. Logan is at her side in an instant, shrieking at Morgeaux, "He's just a child! He's just a child!"

"He was a vampire," Morgeaux replies coolly, tucking her gun again into the waistband of her jeans at the small of her back.

"Charlie! Charlie, can you hear me?" Logan, kneeling over her head, wipes the spurt of blood away but more comes.

She can only gurgle in response, her hands clutching her throat.

"Charlie?" Morgeaux says, rushing to join Logan at her side.

She closes her eyes and focuses her thoughts the way Dr. Larkin taught her in the infirmary, the warm of her own life pooling around her. She concentrates on slowing the flow of her blood and directing it to her throat.

Looks worse than it is, she remembers him saying, shaking his head. *Not good, but not as bad is it seems, right?*

She feels the ends of the wound sealing with the sharp of sear and moving inward along the slice, almost like dominos being knocked down a line from both ends. Within a moment that feels like too many, the wound closes. Her eyes flutter open, her field of vision greeted by Morgeaux and Logan, both with mouths agape. Logan's cheeks are wet with tears.

Morgeaux checks her pulse. "She's still with us. Charlie, can you hear me?"

She tries to nod but closes her eyes as it feels like the ground slips from underneath her.

"It wasn't a deep bite, but deep enough you would've died if—if whatever just happened hadn't happened. How do you feel?"

"Dizzy," she groans. "It'll pass, but I need help to the car."

"It'll pass?!" Logan exclaims. "Charlie, what just happened?"

"Their blood is still in me, or its power, at least. Some of it. I—I don't know, entirely, but that's my guess. It's a trick Dr. Larkin had me practice in the infirmary, concentrating my blood to where I need it. He said it wouldn't last forever, but a little while, at least."

"Thank God for that!" Morgeaux exclaims, gesturing for Logan to help her help Charlie to stand. "That kid got you good."

"I kind of forgot he was there," she sighs. "And you! That gun—"

"Wooden bullets," Morgeaux explains. "I'm not as good a shot as you, though."

Logan furrows his brow as they drag-carry Charlie to the car and get her into the backseat. Morgeaux takes the driver's seat. Logan climbs in the back with Charlie and puts his arm around her, pulling her to lie on his lap.

"So, where to?" Morgeaux asks.

"Home," Charlie answers.

"Rest, Charlie. We'll get you to a hospital. Right, Morgeaux?" But the question from Logan isn't really a question.

"Not a hospital," Charlie says. "I don't want to answer questions and I don't know what they'll find and besides, I'm fine. I'm tired, but I'm fine. See?" She tips her head back where the gash left only scar. "No more bleeding."

"What about the blood you lost?"

"It looked like more than it was. Like Morgeaux said, I would've bled out with time, but it wasn't too deep. He didn't get a good enough bite—"

Logan puts his hands up in surrender, already feeling queasy from her description. "Alright! Alright." He knows from their time at the ranch and coming up against her in countless arguments that he won't win and, besides, she did seem okay.

"No hospital—right now. We'll head home, but we'll monitor how you're feeling, okay?"

She nods sleepily at this, murmuring something unintelligible as her eyes close and her breathing deepens, the rise-fall of her chest slow and steady in a matter of minutes. He rests his arm around her and his head on the window, closing his eyes, following her into slumber as Morgeaux drives—not caring where, so long as it's away.

18

Before

SLIP, SLIP, SLIP: THE SOUND OF SLIPPERS ON THE cold stone floor as a young woman scurries around behind Ismae, changing bed linens, stoking the fire, refilling the water pitcher. And then she's gone, leaving Ismae alone to watch over the thousands of mortal men camped in the countryside beneath the wall where she's turned a guard tower into a bedchamber.

Her decoy rests in her marriage bed, slumbering the night away as mortals often do. Some nights her mortal army practices formations with her real army, those she's Ushered to fight alongside her though they know not she will take up sword with them, her identity obscured by armor. Her mortal army trains often with her Everlasting army, in preparation for when they must go through the Becoming and replace those she's lost.

But tonight their fires burn and they drink and eat and pour over maps in anticipation of what will come. After many years of being left alone to rule, other Everlasting in neighboring territories have taken an interest in hers. Still, it's as close to a night of peace as many have seen in a long while—and only some will see—so she lets them enjoy it.

A knock at the door startles her from reverie.

"Yes?" she calls out, turning from the window to receive the visitor in her private chambers, a breach of etiquette and one that raises questions, but she has no interest in expending energy to beat down ridiculous accusations by chambermaids who keep themselves entertained with gossip.

The door opens slowly and a man with short dark hair and a week's stubble shadowing his chin steps inside holding the gleaming helm of his armor close to his chest and offering a bow, eyes averted as a sign of respect.

"I am sorry to bother m'lady," he starts.

"Come now, look up or you will not be able to see whether I am bothered or not," she interrupts, the command soft.

He looks up, brow furrowed. "M'lady, a scout has returned with some disturbing news. It seems there are ships arriving from the islands in the west."

"And what do they carry?" she asks with a bored sigh.

"Men."

"Warriors or soldiers?"

"I—I'm sorry?" He struggles with the question, unsure of her meaning as he shifts his weight from one foot to the other.

"You are a warrior. Those camped below my wall, they are soldiers. Some of them will die and some of them will be offered life eternal, as you have accepted." She uses the term *accepted* loosely, of course, as her immortal army had little say as she called each into her formal chambers in turn and, with her fangs at their neck, gave them a choice. "It would be wise to act accordingly, warrior," she warns, "so I do not rescind my offer."

"Y—yes m'lady—but, the ships? What would you have us do?"

She turns back to the window. Overhead, the moon casts its glow over the encampment, their dingy tents looking crisp from this distance, their mounts pristine. Though the distance makes them appear as small as ants, their numbers would impress any who would threaten her empire.

And they are not even her Children, whom she has quartered within the castle walls, in barracks and any spare lodging that could be converted into a safe place for them to slumber from dawn to dusk. Ships from the west carry soldiers, not warriors, but she doesn't underestimate the power of numbers.

Still, no need to sacrifice the wheat when the chaff will do.

"What is your name, warrior?"

"Sorenson."

"Sorenson, you will assemble one thousand men from the encampment and lead the ambush to overtake them at the shore. Slaughter them and steal their ships. They be but soldiers, but do not underestimate them. Command your men to load the enemy dead onto these ships and send what helmsmen you need to steer these into the port of their capital city. They will be captured and their heads put on pikes, so choose wisely."

There, she thinks. *If he lives through it, he'll be stronger for it. If not, we will be stronger for it.*

☙❧

"What about Sorenson?" Hunter asks, lying on his back on the cement vault-bed.

One of many, so many lost to time. He returned

from that siege victorious and earned a promotion. But this is not his story, child, nor even his chapter.

Now

VICTOR ESCORTS ME TO MY OWN SUITE AS DAY-break approaches and he obliges, kissing my forehead before retiring for the day himself.

I sit on my bed, freshly made, the smell of bleached linens heavy even though the housekeeper doesn't usually visit my quarters until Sunday. I asked that she not switch out my bedding if I haven't rested in my own, but she insists that her duties are absolute, nonnegotiable. I find the scent comforting as I lie back, taking up the box he gave me those weeks ago from its resting place on my bedside table. Something sticks out from under the pillow I lean back on. My missing copy of *We Have Always Lived at the Castle.* I smile and toss it beside me on the bed. He found it.

Though I opened the box the night he gave it to me, I couldn't bring myself to dig into the contents—photos, notes, trinkets. I take up the photo on top, a young boy that could be Victor and a young girl that could be me smiling at an aquarium. More like those, sometimes with more children, sometimes adults, the locations changing: two houses which I assume to have been ours, a zoo, museum, pool, playground, campground, school. A twinge of familiarity tugs at synapses in my brain, like when you can't remember a word but you know you know it and still it won't reveal itself. Tears fall onto my lap, my lungs filling with the deep breaths that accompany sobs even though the sobs themselves don't come.

The children in the photos grow older, unmistakably us, notes and cards and missives tucked in between: dresses and tuxes, corsages, cars, beer cans, graduation caps, and gowns. I can't bring myself to read the scrawl on the in-between, two distinct handwritings making up the bulk of them. One: scratchy and uneven, as if hurried. The other, mine: slanted just slightly to the right, graceful and slow.

I don't think it then, but later I will wonder how he has all this, why the things he wrote to me would be in this box, too. Instead, I think I see *love* on a few of them but flip quickly past. Then the photos and correspondence stop.

The thing I've been avoiding stares at me now: a jewelry box, red velvet, hinged. Knowing what's inside doesn't quell the heavy pooling in my gut, but looking feels like something that can't be undone once done, so I replace the lid on the box and set it next to me, taking up my worn copy of *We Have Always Lived at the Castle* instead.

I flip to the dog-eared corner marking my last read page when a scrap of paper flutters out. Handwriting, neither scratchy and uneven nor slanting to the right.

You are not alone. There's something you've forgotten you've lost that you need to find. Walk tall and carry a big purse: come nightfall, you'll be in danger.

An informant? I had assumed I was the only Keeper here—just as I had assumed Zeke and I were the only two infiltrating the Praedari as we set up the raid. I didn't find out until too late about Brittany. How could I fail to notice again?

I let the book fall closed as I spring up from my bed to the purse Victor returned to me the night he gave me the box. It's remained draped over the chair of the desk, untouched, since. I grab it and dump the contents onto the desk. Liam and Mina's arm rings clink, metal on metal, hard and unfamiliar, but everything else is as I packed it before I left Caius and the Council to come here, save for the missing cash and cellphone.

I'm about to throw the purse on top of the heap when I feel something I hadn't felt before: a small hard cube in the corner of the fabric. I turn it inside out, the tear in the lining larger than last time I bothered to look but then I never mended it, nor paid it much mind. Now I plunge farther into it, fingers groping for what's lost within. Something velvety-soft that I can't quite grab with just three fingers so I let the tear widen as I wiggle the object with my other hand towards my outstretched fingers which finally wrap around it.

In pulling it through I rip the lining further, now an eight-inch gash of *I don't care* as I study my prize: a navy velvet hinged box, much like the red one I've avoided opening but this time I do not hesitate, Temperance's gift gleaming up at me with its mirrored surface. Not an informant, but the Council? How could they get a message to me without someone on the inside? I take between my fingers a small, mirrored, triangular brooch, sort of like a crude mountain with flowered vines coiling upward, intricate in its detail which one would expect of Temperance, but simple in its construction—nothing flashy, nothing expensive about it, but pretty.

This, I cannot explain: I find myself in the bathroom, in front of the mirror. I pull down on the neck of my top, my skin reflected in the smooth glass. I watch myself unclasp the pin of the brooch from the silken lining of the box. I watch myself hold the brooch as I study my reflection in the mirror. I watch myself as I bring the brooch to my chest, pushing the sharp tack into my flesh, a drop of blood rising to the surface but I do not stop. I watch as the brooch grows hot, a second of flare and sizzle as it melts into my flesh, embedding there.

Took you long enough, and I try to answer, instead collapsing into the deep black of slumber, only vaguely aware of my head hitting the tile of the bathroom floor as day breaks.

Before

A RIDER APPROACHES BUT ISMAE DOES NOT STAND, only peers up into his gray features. Not gray like the color, but gray like stone, like what's indistinct between pebbles as a creek bubbles over them, an invisible veil obscuring everything she could possibly remember about him.

(Of course, dear reader, she could never forget him, nor the others.)

"A Council assembled, and bid I bring you to them."

"To face execution on charges of treason against

whichever sovereignty I've offended?" Her voice more of a growl, her fangs bared.

"No. They wish to speak with you as peer."

"And you act as their messenger? Do they not know we kill diplomatic envoys in these lands?"

"I do not. I am one of the Council. I am called Enoch."

21

Now

I POKE THE BROOCH EMBEDDED IN MY FLESH BEFORE pulling on my shirt, cursing silently at Temperance for not warning me about her gift. Tugging on it only caused pain. Leave it to her to permanently bedazzle an ally. I roll my eyes.

After the whoosh of my suite door opening, I see Victor in his doorway sending Pierce away with a firm handshake. Victor smiles and waves me over when he sees me. Pierce heads in my direction, his mouth pursed just slightly, his eyes unblinking as they catch mine in passing. I glare, the predator within me rising just to snarl before bedding back down.

"Delilah! I'm glad you're up." Victor steps out of his doorway to greet me with a hug. "Pierce is sending Lydia your way."

"Ugh, why?" I don't bother hiding my contempt.

"*Because* she's your security detail, remember?" he reminds me lightly. "And there's something I want her to show you, the final piece to all of this— but I'll meet you guys out there as soon as I finish up this other thing, promise."

I scowl, more harsh of an expression than I intend but he just laughs. "Come on. You're worried about Hunter, right? The tall kid? This is your chance to see that he's just fine."

"You're having Lydia take me to him? Why?" Suspicion rises in my voice like smoke during a fire before I can quell it.

He sighs. "Actually, I messed up. That's why Pierce came by—it turns out that I never should've brought the kids here. They have no part in any of this. The *why* of it won't make sense until I show you something, but I'm releasing him and Kiley tonight with my apologies. They're welcome to stay, as you've chosen to, or to go. Lydia!" He waves at someone behind me down the hall. "Speak of the devil! Lydia here has a bit of a rapport with the kids, so I'm hoping she can help me in my apology?"

"Sure! Pierce filled me in. Kiley's excited, I just came from telling her." A bright voice replies, stepping up too close beside me. "What's she doing here though?" Lydia indicates me with a jerk of her head, the hostility in her tone sharp like a needle in the eye, though Victor doesn't notice or pretends not to.

"I want you to take her with you. You don't mind, right? She feels guilty—" I open my mouth to protest, but he raises his hand to stop me. "You think I don't know you after all these years, Delilah? You need to see for yourself he's fine." I don't argue. Lydia smirks and I growl.

"Not at all!" says Lydia. I can't help but notice

the too-big hunting knife sheathed at the girl's thigh and the sneer she turns into a smile, but I say nothing.

Before

"**Y**OU WISH ME TO SERVE AS YOUR WARLORD?" Ismae scoffs, standing behind the high-backed chair offered her, her back to them as she stares out a window at the hushed hustle of night-time beneath them. Six others, including the one called Enoch, study her from their seats around an ornately carved table. A large goblet rests in front of each, and in front of the seat meant for her, the metallic scent of blood hanging thick in the air. A pewter pitcher sits in front of the man who speaks.

"It is a prestigious appointment," this man to Enoch's left explains. "You would have a seat at this

Council, an equal voice in all matters brought to our attention." In his statement she can hear the unspoken: *as equal a voice as befits a woman.*

"This Council!" She spins on her heels to face the men. "A fledgling government ruling a cultural and political faction still in its infancy," she challenges. "And, pray tell, what would you ask of me in return for such a *prestigious* appointment?"

"Only that you abide by the tenets we've come to agree upon and henceforth expect upheld by all Everlasting—"

"You wish me to hide, as they've chosen to." She gestures to the window behind her with a wide sweep of her arm. "To conceal my nature from those loyal to me." She turns again to gaze out the window. "Why bother to bid me here?"

"Your tactical acumen has not gone unnoticed. Exceptional, as found in a woman—and such that rivals our own," a voice she doesn't recognize explains.

Then Enoch says, "You are correct that one of

our founding principles—and, after much discussion, the one we hold most sacred as a Council—is to remain hidden. We believe humanity is not ready to know of our existence. Perhaps in time—"

"I do not rule from the shadows. I rule from the trenches."

"Ismae—"

But she faces the first man once again, regarding him coolly. "You may address me as Empress, as that is my title by right and by rule."

His lips purse and he spins the signet ring on his finger twice before offering a tight-lipped smile. "As you wish, *Empress*. The mortals need us—to provide for them, to guide them, to protect them. Plague, famine, religious upheaval—"

"And yet none of this has touched my empire since the death of my husband. Since *before* his death, when I took command of his armies as his betrothed."

"Yet."

"Is that a threat?" She steps towards the table,

folding her hands on the curved back of the chair meant for her.

"It is a fact. You're as vulnerable as we are—more so, as you rule openly, your nature known to all."

"You would be wise to speak more carefully. I suffer not an uncivil tongue, nor a threat. Not only have we remained stalwart in the face of plague, famine, and religious upheaval, but my armies have repeatedly vanquished the armies of my enemies, *your* armies, successfully absorbing those survivors who atone for their transgressions." Though she offers this as known fact, they know not how few survive the Rite of Atonement—and that those who *do* survive do not remain unchanged forever by it.

"Do not get cocky—"

"Please. Your ego summoned me to these chambers. You say you wish to protect the mortals, but from what, exactly? Your fear of them, perhaps?"

"You began your rule from the shadow of your husband's throne. It would be wise to continue your rule from the shadow of the throne of the children you have not borne," another Councilman finally speaks up, tone sharp.

"Spoken like a man who commands many swords but has never lifted even one. You brought me this far to offer advice, or an ultimatum?"

"We are more than our numbers here. We have the sworn fealty of the first of the Everlasting pledging loyalty to the newly founded Keepers, their support bolstered by the empires they rule and the armies they command."

"It is lucky you count amongst the Keepers more than just those assembled here, for I will not serve you, now or ever—as your Warlord or otherwise."

The man to the left of the one called Enoch taps his signet ring on the wooden table twice. The two men to either side of her stand and like dominos each of the others at the table follow, the man with the ring standing last. Ismae snarls and pulls from the folds of her skirt two imperfect shafts of wood, polished to gleaming and darker than most of the wood native to this region.

A laugh bubbles from the open mouth of the man with the ring, cut short as she plunges one of the stakes into the chest of the man nearest her who erupts into a cloud of ash, a feral glint in her eyes. She spins to the other man who was seated next to her, her leg sweeping his out from under him, knees buckling. He falls to his back on the floor with a grunt and she follows him, her knees digging into the soft of his belly on impact as she drives a stake into his dead heart.

Someone grabs her as she finds herself kneeling in ashy remains, the wild thing inside her all claws and snapping jaw as her assailant flings her against the wall, her turn to grunt. Another man lunges for her and she spins against the wall, sidestepping him so he would collide face-first with the wall were it not for the stake her outstretched arm held in waiting. As soon as she feels the force of his impaling himself on her stake, she lets go, leaping onto the table at the center of the room before she hears the stake clatter to the stone floor.

Three men circle her: two she doesn't know and the one called Enoch. The two scramble to climb up onto the table, one with ease and the other having grabbed the stake she's dropped, Enoch hanging back. Ismae bites the stake she still holds between her teeth and jumps, reaching above her to grab the modest wheel chandelier. With a powerful kick of her legs out and forward, she propels herself over one of the men as he stands up on the table. Before he can pivot to face her, she shoves the stake through his back and out his chest. The other man on the table lunges through the cloud of ash that was his Council-mate without missing a beat, shoving Ismae again to her back as his stake glances off her chest. He recovers quickly, now straddling her, her arms pinned beneath his knees momentarily. He raises the stake above her with both hands, plunging it downwards through her and into the table below.

His eyes widen, mirroring hers as the stone at her throat glows. His surprise allows her to wriggle her wrists free. She grabs the stake in her chest with both hands, pulling it slowly from the sheath of her flesh and bone and muscle with a terrifying howl. Channeling the strength of the predator within her with another howl, she drives the stake blunt-end first into his dead heart.

She swings her legs over the edge of the table and drops to the floor, staring at the last Council member.

"You, Enoch. Tell your Keepers what happened here. Tell them me and my army will be waiting for them—for eternity, if we must."

23

Now

THE PREDATOR WITHIN ME STIRS BEFORE WE EVEN
reach the bottom of the stone stairs. Lydia
hasn't said a word to me, leading in silence. The
thing within me ignores the girl, and has, for the
most part, since our first encounter after Johnny's
disappearance, save for when rising to meet the
thing inside *her.*

No, something inside me catches the scent of
something mostly unfamiliar—not the boy, his
unwashed stench of sweat and fear reminiscent of
the one time I met him, before I had to turn on
them to preserve my own cover. This thing, like sea

and waterlily, but as if through moss as we descend into the damp of earth.

It's not only that I smell the sea, but that I feel it well up underneath me, as thick and full as molasses. Some might describe it as the feeling that time has slowed, but that's not accurate: it's as if everything in the universe marches on at its own perfect pace, kept as clockwork, while I find myself heavy—a mosquito perched, oblivious, on the side of a tree as the stick of a drop of sap rolls down the bark towards it. Sap isn't a predator. The bark is not a trap. And yet the mosquito is swallowed up, preserved.

24

Before

"YOU ARE FREE MEN HERE," ISMAE SHOUTS OVER the din of the legions she's Ushered, knowing only those nearest her can hear her words, but the bards will make sure to carry her message between camps. From atop her black mount, she surveys thousands of men, miles of men, each in the garb of their respective units from their respective armies, the armies they once fought in and for, most holding tight to the traditions they had taken from them when her enemies invaded their lands. Her empire became something of a refuge for those who had everything stripped from them. While she demanded nothing less than complete loyalty, she offered them a parcel of land and the privacy to worship and live as they pleased and in return they defended their new homeland with fervor.

"Free men! Gifted of the Blood of your Empress," she repeats, her words met with a roar of approval. Her horse rears up once, twice, as if a dance, and she holds the reins loosely. "And for that freedom I demand a price: that you defend it, that you do not squander it. My enemies of the Blood would seek to overtake us, to strip from you your land, your Gods, your love, your life—my enemies who are *your* enemies. And now they throw their mortal armies at us, seeking to extinguish our way of life."

Wind howls through the night-dark countryside, beating the likewise dark silks of her gown against her dead skin and lifting her hair, creating a sort of whipping, living mane framing her face. She looks out over the horizon where stars bejewel the tapestry of night, their beauty a blessing she recognizes even in this moment, *especially* in this moment.

"But I misspoke!" she continues. "You are not *men*, and do not let them call you such—you, my Children, are *more than men*! You are my Blood! You are Everlasting! You are immortal! You are to them their Gods made manifest!"

Loud howling and the stamping of thousands of heavy-footed soldiers ripple through her assembled legions, herself the center point, the cacophony radiating outward from her. She lets it move outward from her before speaking again.

"We do not seek to conquer, for we have no need of their lands or their ships." Her words drip with disgust. "But let them come, my Children! Let them come and find a good death by your hand, your sword, your fangs. Send them into whatever afterlife their Gods promise them. Let them come, let them raise arms against us. Let them threaten your children as they threaten you, *my* Children—and then let their blood nourish our soil so your crops may flourish. Let their entrails feed our pigs so your children eat well this winter. Let them watch as ghosts from their eternal rest as we do not pillage their villages, do not rape their women, do not punish their children for their fathers' ill-placed loyalty."

"But enough of what we will not do!" She raises a sword, the heft of which would cause even the strongest of her mortal army difficulty. "Enemies of the Blood deliver to us a sea of crimson. Drink deep, my Children, drink well!" She punctuates this by thrusting the sword in the air, her mount rearing up as if to dance to the raucous that follows with its own loud whinny.

It was the last of their assaults against us, and all that came before doesn't matter. Only what came after. That's all anyone remembers, anyhow.

"Why?" Hunter asks.

Because history only remembers mistakes.

25

Now

KEY RATTLES IN A LOCK, A SOUND I HAVEN'T heard since arriving at the facility. Down here they haven't bothered with technology. A grunt as Lydia heaves open the door and that's when it rushes over me: a swell of earth from below me and I'm thrown to the bottom few stone stairs as if by a ghost. I'm vaguely aware of a third figure kneeling inside the room next to a large cement vault that I can't look away from, unmoving, staring.

Voices, indistinct, as if through water. The smell of my blood awakens the predator within me, a mess of gnashing teeth and a snarl and a voice emerges over the din of it all: *See!* And with that command I see, I see the all of it—past and present and future knotting in my gut, hundreds of thousands of lives and unlives lost, billions still hanging in the balance or maybe those are stars? I see the web of red thread that connects Ismae and Zeke and me and that spiders from me outward to Victor, Lydia, Hunter, Kylie, Logan, Charlie, Morgeaux, Quinn, Liam and Mina, the Council of Keepers, Caius, Simone, Tomas, Brittany, my old pack—people I haven't met or will meet or could meet or maybe they're just stars?

A constellation amasses in my gut, mythic figures coming to unlife and fighting, determining what stories will be worshipped and which lost. Every story starts somewhere, in a seed of truth. A searing pain in my chest. *See! See! See!* And I can't unsee. A glimpse into the now and I can feel the voices I cannot hear, each syllable like a gunshot, their scrambling around me as I writhe and convulse. A moment of clarity swallowed up.

Before

THERE ISMAE STANDS, BLOOD-DRENCHED, BARE hands clutching the sloppy entrails of another just like her, one of the Everlasting. The wind relentless, kicking up the heavy skirts of her gown, her hair matted to her head. The battlefield now covered in the thick muck of ash and blood and bodily shrapnel of those fallen but not quite dead, those left encircling her, closing the distance between themselves and their progenitor, their mother. In an instant she spins on one who's crept behind her, unaware that though she doesn't see him she needn't see him; in the next his comrade's intestines, still attached to an opened gut, are wrapped once, twice, three times around his throat as she pulls in opposite directions, hard enough in a single tug to choke the breath from a mortal but that's not her objective, that's not good enough, so she keeps pulling. Amazing, the strength of something meant to stay tucked away in this weak fortress of flesh, hidden in our guts. The sinewy muscle cuts into the throat of the man whose hot life force gushes forth, spraying her but indistinguishable from the blood of hundreds as nameless as he, to whom she lent the gift of immortality only to take it again in an instant.

Ismae the Bloody awakens face down in the cooling putrid sludge of ash and blood, alone, and weeps. The predator within slinks, satisfied, to a far corner of her soul and, though she has no recollection of the past few hours, a feeling like molten iron knots in her gut and builds up the skeleton of a cage around her heart. She can taste their blood, the metallic choir that sang on her tongue and down her throat. These were the people who were willing to give their lives to protect what she'd built. And they had. After all, the empire could not support so many predators.

At her throat, the Stone of Nyx hangs matte and black, spent.

27

Now

HANDS ON ME, DRAGGING ME. I'M ON A BATTLE-
field, or what's left of it, littered with limbs
and the dead and the ash of undeath. Now a sea
of red sludge, a thick ash-blood slurry, a flood I've
brought down on us all. I kneel, cup my hands and
lift some to my mouth. I am the sky weeping, as
when they told me of Zeke, my howls echoing like
crashing waves in sea-cave.

A glass coffin.

Inside, Snow White.

Inside, poison apple on her breath.

(I'm too late.)

I throw my head back and gulp blood-water from the sky that I am and am not, but sputter dirt and now I'm clawing, clawing, clawing from a grave no dead dare rest in.

I've taken lives, mortal and Everlasting, though I've never wept for them. Each of their lives a droplet of the blood-water I gulp, wept by the sky. How easily we find ourselves reduced to the stick of sap, a pile of ash, buried by either.

I didn't watch Liam and Mina greet the sun. (I'm too late.) As candles burn, wax drips, pooling at the base. Grab it quickly enough—not molten, but not solid—and it can be shaped into something, preserved, kept. Useless as garbage.

28

Now

"Y OU KILLED THEM. YOU KILLED THE ONES YOU made. That's like—that's like what? Like when a mother in the wild eats her young? Except . . . you were human once. They were human once," Hunter continues, staring ahead as if in a trance, unaware of the intrusion.

It was necessary. The newly-formed Keepers were wrong about the need to hide, at least then. Mortals weren't the greatest threat to our existence: we were. So many were Ushered out of vanity, a sense of entitlement, narcissism. Others were Ushered to be used as political pawns, or as punishment for some slight or offense committed by themselves or someone close to them. Still others were rewarded with immortality for their loyalty, or by a lover who wished them by their side forever. Overpopulation loomed, and in my empire this disease started and ended with me.

I failed, though, for I did not kill them all. I'd Ushered too many, and my empire sprawled far beyond what walls we started within. We flourished, but how does the forest swallow an errant strike of lightning? I allowed us to become vulnerable and, as a result, wild-fire erupted: we burned the Keepers, starting with their Council and raging through the armies sent in retribution. The thing about wildfire, though? It's difficult to control, to predict. Fire can jump, can shift direction without notice. The time came that I turned on my Children, but flames alone do not bear the burden of destruction. What's left behind, the smoke and ash and debris, the devastation: but even from this seemingly-barren ash of wildfire can something grow.

Enoch did as he was asked and it did not take long for my surviving Children to learn what fate met the

Council of Keepers when they asked their Usher to join them as Warlord at the cost of all their freedom. My Children rose up, stronger, somehow than before and with renewed purpose. Like a dormant seed awakening to colonize a burn site, gardens were dedicated to me as temples and the first of the Praedari born. They swore fealty to me again, this time as my Children, as my Blood. Where once I offered them immortality with my fangs at their throat, it now felt as if their fangs were at mine, demanding I mother their revolution.

So I did, by remaining silent. I no longer hunted my remaining Children. By returning to the walls I'd once constructed to contain us, I found solace in isolation. When those walls finally crumbled, I left. I put seas and then oceans between my Children's gardens and my own but their fervor did not diminish. The Praedari grew from cult status, rising up as nearly equal in power to the Keepers. Their traditions mirrored those of their enemy, but something feral unnamed underscored their rites. The Keepers persecuted the Praedari as heretics even then, their dreams *of unifying the Everlasting to protect themselves from your mortal world spilled as blood in countless battles. Eventually the Keepers rose to dual purpose: to protect themselves from humanity and to protect humanity from the Praedari.*

You liken me to something wild eating her young. You think I did not mourn those I killed? I did, and I Ushered no other for centuries—but the darkest of my mourning did not eclipse until I led Ezekiel's Rite of Binding.

29

Now

"YOU'RE SURE, SIREN?"

"I am. The girl has been brought to Ismae the Bloody. I've seen the beginning of the end."

"Then we move?"

Five heads turn to the Eldest of them: Enoch the Gray. From the head of the table he offers no spoken reply, merely a nearly imperceptible dip of his head in assent.

30

Now

*H*E KNOWS *I* NEED YOUR HEART AND LUNG, *Childe, don't you see? He's sent you here to die.*

But before I can answer there's a rumbling off in the distance, outside this cellar, outside this storm I've become: the siege has begun.

I do not know this yet, of course.